ROYAL BY DESIGN

CHAPTER 1

10 YEARS EARLIER

"You may have two biscuits."

Finley put the cover back on the fancy, talking jar and took the next one down from the high shelf. "You may have one biscuit." He shook his head and replaced the empty jar taking down the third.

The staff had tidied up the guest living room for him again this year, and he wasn't sure if he could touch anything but wondered what this one said. Would they have to clean up after him again? He didn't love the idea of making more work for the poor souls. At home, he was the cleaning staff, and it felt weird having people doing things for him.

Adrian ran in, full of energy as always. He usually had to play a proper prince, but when it was the two of them, he could just be a kid. Adrian was a year younger than him. The two had become instant friends when they'd met at camp when they were seven and eight. Thick as thieves and twice as mischievous. Once they'd outgrown camp, Adrian began inviting Finley to his family home for the summers—a palace, where his mum and pa ruled the land of Ixica.

His friend bounced on his toes and his eyes fastened on the object Finley still held. "Whoa! The old treat jars. I haven't seen those in forever! Now that we're older, we no longer need the jar telling us what we can eat. That's fantastic. Put it up. Come on, let's go out riding."

He placed the canister back on the shelf in the guest living room where in a normal home it could collect dust and raced after Adrian through the hallways. They almost ran into Malcolm, who glared at them. "Not you again! I thought as of last summer we were done with enduring your tortures. How long do we have to put up with you?"

Finley paused for a moment, just staring at Malcolm, who, as always, looked perfect. Not a hair out of place, his clothes immaculate; even his glare was stunning. The fire in his eyes felt like a challenge. Finley smirked and missed Adrian's comeback to Malcolm as he stared at the man. He grabbed Adrian's hand and dragged him towards the stairs. Slipping out of the palace, they ran to the stables and waited for mounts to be saddled for them.

Finley had ridden since he was young. His family wasn't wealthy or royalty like Adrian's, but his aunt and uncle owned a farm and he'd spent time riding. He preferred losing himself on the computer, but horses were fun, too. He figured his parents allowed him to come to Ixica because, while there, he socialized with real people instead of their avatars. They also liked having time without a kid around.

Once they made it to the trail in the woods, Finley turned to his friend. "I have a great idea for tonight."

Adrian narrowed his eyes. "Why do I have a feeling you're about to get me in trouble?"

He tried to keep a blank face, but feared he failed. "Would I get you in trouble, mate?"

Rubbing his hand over his face, Adrian sighed. "Every chance you get. Is it Malcolm again? You always go after Malcolm."

Finley shrugged. "Princess Anastasia will be the next Queen…and in all honesty, she kind of scares me. Who else is there? The King? The Queen? Sidney?" He shivered at the mere thought of pranking the royal advisor. "I think not. That leaves your brother."

Adrian laughed. "I don't see why you're afraid of Star; she's way nicer than Malcolm. But okay, talk to me. What's this big idea of yours?"

They discussed plans as their horses walked through

the shade of the trees on a circuitous route. The birds sang a background soundtrack to their scheming. It made Finley feel like a star in a film. By the time they returned, their plans for an evening of hijinks had solidified.

Adrian's suite of rooms was across the hall from Malcolm's. They went into the sitting room and buzzed for a servant. Adrian requested balloons. While they waited, Adrian shook his head. "Do you have other big plans for the summer besides terrorizing my brother?"

With a shrug, Finley flopped back on the couch. "I'd like to learn a new programming language. My parents' goal in me coming here is to get me away from the computer, but I'm hoping the librarian can find this book I've been searching for. Otherwise, there are some great websites that can teach me the basics of what I want to learn."

"I can ask my pa to set up a computer in your room for when you're in your lessons."

He sat up with the excitement of the summer bubbling up in him. No one to stop his plans from coming to fruition, both technological and social. "There are some other ideas I have for sneaky fun we can have...I learned a few recipes. Did you know the kind of items you can bake into a cake?"

Adrian shot up, leaning forward with interest. "You can bake?"

Finley nodded. "I can. Just about anything. It's saved the family loads of money having me do all the festive baking each year. But I figured we may be able to have a bit of fun with your parents with some silly treats…if you think that would be okay."

Adrian's eyes twinkled with agreement. They continued to plan other shenanigans past the delivery of the balloon for the current night's activity. They filled the balloons with water, then arranged the water bombs on Malcolm's bed.

After dinner, they decided they'd make the surprise treats in a few days, once Finley had time to secure all the right ingredients. The two sat on the bed cross-legged with Finley's laptop between them, searching for the books he wanted to ask the librarian about. It was a small computer that wouldn't do much; all his family would allow him.

Adrian was ignorant about computers, the internet, and programming languages. Finley described how the different aspects of a website worked and what he did to circumnavigate the protections. He explained what he'd do if he could build the computer of his dreams with more power than the tiny laptop had. Everything he'd do once he had money of his own.

They were just getting to a site about security when a scream came from across the hall.

CHAPTER 2

3 YEARS EARLIER

"**M**alcolm Tuffin!" the voice boomed out, reverberating across the auditorium.

Malcolm sauntered across the stage in his black cap and gown and shook the hands of each of the officials at the other end of the stage. He'd done it! Despite what everyone thought, he was graduating from college.

After the pomp and circumstance, his family took him out to dinner, a French restaurant with a private area where they could eat without being seen. He'd graduated in England. Although recognition was less likely, it was still possible, so the family preferred a private room.

His father sipped his wine. "Now, Malcolm, I'm proud of you. You've always been a joy to me, but graduating college is quite the achievement." The group raised their glasses with a cheer.

Malcolm took a quick sip of wine.

Anastasia took a bite of black olive tapenade. "I'm just shocked you graduated in four years. How did you finish your homework with all the parties?"

Malcolm glared at her, then winked. "I'll have you know, I studied and kept my grades up. Maybe not as well as you, but enough to do the family proud."

With a big smile, Adrian served up some tartare de Filet de Boeuf to his plate. They'd decided to share an appetizer. "I just hope that one day I can be as honorable as you, Malcolm."

"I bask in the love you all give me on this day of my graduation. Four years of hardship and toil, only to be harassed by my family at the end."

Adrian laughed. "Harassed! I can only imagine what you'll do to me in two years. And do you even remember Anastasia's graduation last year? Oh, your selective memory. I do wonder how many professors let you pass for your good looks and pity for attempting to charm them." Finished with his razzing, he took another bite of the tartare.

Pa chuckled. "It is nice to be away from the palace and able to just be a family. We don't do this enough."

A week later, Malcolm stood in the foyer of his home in Ixica, the royal palace. He'd been home a few days and he was about to go to the shop owned by Casimir, a fashion designer…*the* fashion designer in Ixica, and hoped the man would meet with him. Everyone else in the family was busy. It was why he'd selected this time; he knew he wouldn't run into anyone. Butterflies danced in his stomach. He checked to make sure he had his bag and portfolio, then headed out to his car.

He wasn't sure if he'd be asked to show his work, or perform any tasks, but he wanted to be prepared for anything. This was the most important interview of his life.

His worry shifted to excitement for a moment as he stared at his new car. For graduation, his parents let him choose any car he wanted, and he picked out a green Aston Martin Rapide named Sage Nightstar. He loved his new car and wouldn't let anyone else drive her. He put his portfolio of work and the bag in the trunk and slid into the front seat.

No one else, beyond his security detail, knew about this meeting with Casimir, this job interview. He hadn't told his parents, his siblings, no one. None of them would understand. If he got the job, he'd have to figure out what to tell people because this wasn't the kind of occupation the royal family would understand or support.

He drove up to the storefront of the most famous fashion house in all of Ixica and gazed at the beautiful designs in the window. His stomach churned with nerves as he gathered his stuff. Casimir expected him, but he'd only made an appointment to see him, he hadn't explained why. *Am I embarrassed? Do I think he'll laugh me out of his design studio? Face it, Malcolm, the real reason you didn't tell the designer the truth was you didn't think he'd see you if he knew.*

Firming his resolve, Malcolm entered the store and went to the back where he was to meet the design expert. Casimir waited for him in the large studio, tables filled with a rainbow assortment of fabric. A sewing machine in the back hummed—perhaps one of his assistants hard at work. Malcolm marveled at the designs plastered on the walls. He gaped in awe at everything as he entered the workspace. The weight of Casimir's knowledge and expertise seemed to fill the room. Such genius. He felt lost in the magnitude of all he saw.

"Prince Malcolm, you come bearing gifts. How can I be of service to you and your family on this fine day?"

Malcolm stood frozen for a moment, taking in Casimir with his shoulder-length, wavy brown hair, brown eyes, and immaculate dress. He presented himself as if prepared for dining at the palace with the King and Queen. Nerves playing havoc with his ability to speak, Malcolm licked his lips and finally managed to take a breath. "These aren't gifts, sir. I would like to talk with you—in private if possible."

He'd never felt so small and scared in his life. He didn't recognize his own voice. He'd spoken to professors with more force and aplomb. But he'd never wanted anything more than this. *God, I want this job. Is there a job to be had? Please let there be a job! Working for the premier designer and artist in all Ixica would be a dream! Please don't mess this up.*

Casimir tilted his head. "We can talk here. Anything you say can be said in front of my worker bees; they are completely trustworthy."

Doubt assailed him, but he nodded. Malcolm placed his portfolio on a clear area of the worktable near Casimir and gulped in some air. He'd prepared a list of talking points—like Sidney had taught him and his siblings—written them down and memorized a key word for each. He had to get through the list in a calm, succinct manner.

He stood a bit taller and tried to harness his nervous energy. "I recently graduated from the University of Cambridge and earned a degree in fashion design. My family doesn't know which classes I took. I have a portfolio of my work and would like a job apprenticing with you."

One of Casimir's elegant brows rose.

As if struck by lightning, Malcolm realized he forgot a main point. He held up his hands. "Before looking at my work or making any decisions, I would ask two things.

First, you don't treat me like a Prince of the royal family. Look at my designs as any other person desperate to work with someone of your caliber. And two, if you do accept me, please don't inform the King and Queen. I'll let them know in my own time."

His heart pounded in his chest like a sledgehammer. *Am I about to faint dead away in the midst of Casimir's fashion kingdom?*

He barely breathed as the man's eyes traveled up and down his casual attire, then, with a tilt of his head, he sighed. "I will evaluate your portfolio, boy, and then probably do what I do with ninety-five percent of the portfolios I see: send you on your way. I will honor your last request and nothing of what happened here will leave this room by my mouth or any of my people's. We are all good at keeping secrets."

Casimir slowly reached out and pulled the flat, gray leather case containing Malcolm's life in art designs closer. The sound of the zipper reverberated through the large room, sending chills down Malcolm's back. He watched, transfixed, as Casimir flipped page after page, gazing down at each image. Some he'd hold up to study, others he passed by with barely a glance. Every page passed was a weight on his gut.

Does he like it? Hate it? Do I have a future here?

By the end, Malcolm's hands trembled, and his mouth was dry. He wasn't sure how much more of the agony he could take, waiting and watching as his possible futures passed in front of his eyes. Dread filled him with its chilled brew as Casimir flipped the last pages of his designs and the master designer faced him. "Well, young Prince, you've surprised me today…and I am not often surprised. You have talent and an eye for design. I'll grant you a three-month probationary trial. After that, we'll sit and decide whether you and I want to continue our relationship as master and apprentice."

Malcolm's muscles turned to Jell-O and he barely remained standing. He wanted to scream in triumph and beat his fist in the air and yell in delight. Instead, he fell back on all the training he'd ever received and smiled. "Thank you, thank you so much, Master Designer Casimir. You'll not regret it."

"I will if you continue calling me that. I'll call you 'Malcolm' while we're here and you're working for me, and you'll call me 'Casimir.' You'll start tomorrow, nine in the morning, sharp. Until tomorrow." He started to look away, then turned back. "Though, I'd be more comfortable if you told your parents."

Panic surged through him, but his mind grasped a solution. "How about my sister? She'll be the next Queen anyway."

He waved a hand. "Princess Anastasia, then. But if the King or Queen finds out, you're taking the fall for this. Now, go, tell her. And I'll see you tomorrow."

Once he arrived home, he found Anastasia and asked

if she'd go riding with him. Since it was one of her favorite pastimes, he knew she'd agree. As their horses were brought out, he noticed a new horse handler, blond with brown eyes…and handsome.

When his horse was close enough to take from the man, he gave the new worker a half-smile. "You're new. To what do I owe the pleasure of your attendance?"

The new stable hand's eyes widened, and he licked his lips. "I requested to bring you your horse, Your Highness, I wanted to get closer to you." A blush colored his face a lovely red.

Malcolm traced the new worker's jaw with a finger. "Well, I'm glad you did. If I'd known you were available, trust me, I'd have requested you, love."

The man's eyes snapped up to his. "My name's Jordan, Your Highness. Request my services any time you'd like."

He leaned down so his mouth was right by Jordan's ear. "Oh, I think I'll have need of many of your services."

"Hurry up, Malcolm, I don't have all day!" Anastasia's voice interrupted from across the stable yard.

CHAPTER 3

PRESENT DAY

Finley sat in his London flat. Code streamed on two of his three monitors as he strove to stay ahead of the tracker security bot. The game had his blood sizzling in his veins and excitement pulsing in his soul. God, he loved his job.

There it was! A small and almost insignificant opening in the company's firewall. His fingers flew over his keyboard. He slipped in, invading the company's kingdom. Spinning in his seat, his hands landed on his secondary keyboard, and he banged away, typing a series of codes and passwords. He sank deeper into the net, seeking the passcode. The code set up for this job, it changed every fifteen minutes. He needed it to prove not only that he'd made it in, but *when* he'd made it in. A digital timestamp.

Finley slid over to his first keyboard and moved through the corridors of the castle—as he thought of the world he'd snuck into—slinking through the walls like a rogue. He located the treasure room, got to the pedestal with the missing jewel, and found the spot to type in the code from the deep net. With a final click, the job he'd been working on for hours—or days?—was complete.

A bell should have been dinging deep in the security office of the company that hired him, indicating that he'd made it in. His phone should be ringing…right…

Ring!

Now.

"Finley Johnson, IT Security Specialist."

"Hey, Fin, It's Adrian." His voice cracked with a soft note he'd never heard from his friend before. "Do you have a minute?"

His phone beeped. The security detail from the company he'd just hacked was trying to get ahold of him, but right now he could care less. He needed the job, the recommendation, but this was Adrian. He'd do anything for him. "For you, mate, I have two. What's up?"

His friend took a shuddery breath. "It's my pa, Fin. He didn't survive. I don't know what I'm doing…what to do."

A chunk of Finley's world cracked and fell away. A tear burned down his cheek. The King had been a second father to him…and he was dead? "I'll be there as fast as I can. I don't know if I can help, but I'll be there." His mind whirled. He could transfer most of his responsibilities to Ixica, but his top priority was Adrian and his family.

A silence followed his words along with a few sniffles. "Thanks, Fin. I…I need to go. Do you want the private jet?"

Finley surveyed all his stuff. "Only if it's coming this way." He didn't want to be a burden. "I have a load of stuff, but I can figure it out—you know me. I don't want to be a bother."

"It will be there to pick you up in four hours. Does that work?"

It felt like a weight had been lifted from his shoulders. "Yes, that would be lovely."

Once Adrian ended the call, Finley returned the call he'd missed and finished off the job he'd been working on.

Once in Ixica, a car waited to pick Finley up. At the palace, he had to adjust to servants and having them help with all his daily needs. They carefully helped him to the guest room he'd come to think of as his over the years.

"Thanks for helping me," he said, rubbing his neck. "I really could've managed, you know. I hate to take up your time."

Trace, one of the maids, smiled warmly up at him. "Anything for you, Master Finley, you're never a burden around here. I'll have the kitchen send up an afternoon tea service since you missed lunch."

He tried to stop her, but she was away before his hand reached waist high.

He sighed and relaxed as he looked around the space he thought of as his. He'd spent summers in these rooms for over ten years. He wasn't even sure if they had other people use this suite when he wasn't around. If he were honest with himself, he feared the answer if he ever braved the question.

His tea and biscuits arrived. "Sir, the family is away right now, and you'll be on your own for dinner. The chef has prepared your favorite, Shepherd's pie with apple clotted cream pie for dessert."

Finley nodded. "Thank the chef for me; that dinner sounds perfect."

After the servant left, he started rearranging his rooms to allow space for his computers and monitors. He decided to use a corner of the bedroom instead of the sitting room; he didn't want every person who came into the room to be tempted to ask him about his setup.

After he ate, he sorted through his emails, deciding if anything was worth his immediate attention. He flagged two new jobs he thought would be quick and easy to finish while away from his more secure home. There was another potential job, but he feared if the security could track him back, he'd be putting the royal family in the scope of the company's attention, and that wasn't acceptable. He kept scrolling.

A knock and the door opening were his only warning that Adrian had returned home. "Finley, you're here!"

Finley jumped up and gave his friend a hug. "I am so sorry about how much this situation sucks. I miss your pa and his funny sense of humor."

Adrian huffed out a laugh. "I know, I can't believe he won't be around to tell any of his jokes and stories."

They pulled apart, and Adrian sat on the bed. "The funerals are tomorrow. First, one in the city for everyone in the country. Then a second one for just the family. You are invited to both, or neither, or whatever you feel is best."

Finley lightly punched Adrian's shoulder before dropping down in his desk chair. "I'm with you, mate. I want to grieve with you. You know he was so much better to me than mine. I feel lost without him, too."

CHAPTER 4

Malcolm and Adrian walked out of the sitting room… well, they'd been kicked out of the room everyone had been occupying. Anastasia had just learned she had to return to America to find the signet ring she'd gifted a girl when she was twelve. He shook his head and sighed, thinking about the circumstances.

I'm pretty sure my sister wasn't going to tell the Queen and her advisor that the ring had been gifted to Jamie all those years ago during our vacation to the U.S. Maybe I shouldn't have told them Anastasia had given her ring away when she was twelve, but someone had to.

They reached the stairs and Adrian placed his hand on Malcolm's arm. "I can't believe you just up and said that. Where were you when we sat through all of those classes on diplomacy?"

He rolled his eyes. "Anastasia will be Queen. You'll be her advisor. I won't be working for the royal family, at least not in any official capacity." As they walked up the steps, he added, "I knew I never really needed to learn all those lessons you and our royal sister painstakingly studied, so I just did the bare minimum to prevent the wrath of Sidney from falling down upon my head."

When they reached the third floor, they found Finley sitting on one of the hallway couches, reading a book. His head snapped up at their approach, and he slipped his book into a pocket. Even in his current state, Malcolm wondered at the trousers with the huge packets. Finley's face softened at seeing Adrian. He darted his focus to Malcolm, almost tensing as if he expected to be yelled at or attacked, before giving all his attention to his brother. "How are you doing? Everything okay?"

Adrian shrugged. "Yeah, it's just been a long day. I'm going to go sit in my room. Do you want to join me?"

Finley seemed to droop. "Sure. I thought we may go riding, get out of here for a bit. Fresh air would be good, but it's up to you."

"I'm sorry, Fin," Adrian sighed with a shrug. "I'm

really not up to that. You can go; I would be fine being alone for a spell."

An air of disappointment flowed over Finley. Malcolm knew he'd give up his plans for Adrian. Malcolm shifted his gaze to his brother. The family had been running around since that morning, and Malcolm could see how tired his brother was. He'd been stepping up, playing interference for both their mother and Anastasia. He could see how some time alone would be really seductive.

On the other hand, Finley had flown out to support the family, and he'd been doing everything an outsider could. No, not an outsider. Finley practically *was* family based on how much everyone leaned on him that day. Despite his help, Adrian and Anastasia kept checking with him to see if he was okay with the crowds. His eyes were a bit wild throughout the day, but he always shook his head, and said he was there for the family.

The man's head looked ready to explode from being around people and inside all day. Malcolm wasn't sure what he did when he wasn't causing havoc and mayhem around the palace, but he guessed it wasn't spending his time in big crowds.

With a sigh, he made his final decision. "I'll go riding with you. Let's give Adrian some rest."

Both Finley and his brother gaped at him, and he laughed. His first real laugh since he'd heard his father had passed. "Come on, trickster, let's go find some horses to ride."

Finley's eyes widened. He stood with a nod and followed. He walked stiffly, but then again, he'd been stuffed in the house all day; who wouldn't be stiff?

When they arrived at the stables, Jordan ran out and saw him with Finley. Eyes wide, the color drained from his face, and he stopped. Suddenly Jordan's face hardened before turning red. He spun on his heel and stormed into the barn. Several minutes later he returned with two saddled and bridled horses. "Your mounts, Your Highness."

He gazed at the stable hand, confused. "Jordan?"

"Is there anything else you'll be needing, Prince Malcolm?"

With a tilt of his head, Malcolm took his reins, confusion and frustration rolling inside him like a stormy sea. "No, thank you."

He and Finley mounted and headed for the shaded paths in the woods east of the palace. Once they were alone, Finley's shoulders dropped. "I'm sorry about that."

Malcolm narrowed his eyes. "About what?"

"Jordan must've thought we were out on a date. The reputation of our relationship amongst the staff…they know I'm Adrian's friend and you only put up with me. And here we are, riding together. I'm sorry if I messed something up."

Replaying the scene, Malcolm slapped his forehead. "No, *I* should be sorry. Hang out too much with me, and

I'll ruin your reputation."

As the silence between them grew, Malcolm glanced over. Finley was blushing. He considered all the reasons why he could be embarrassed. Malcolm realized how little he knew about the man who practically lived at his home every summer for more than ten years. Not wanting to make him feel uncomfortable, he decided to change the subject. "So, now that you aren't running around the palace harassing me, what do you do with all your time?"

As they continued down the trail, Malcolm listened, amazed, learning about Finley's profession as a computer hacker. Instead of doing it illegally, he contracted with companies to test their security systems. He explained how he would continue to work while in Ixica, but nothing big. As he tested systems, companies he worked for, or other hackers, could follow him back if he didn't do his job correctly, and he didn't want to endanger the palace.

"But our security is pretty tight, isn't it?" Malcolm asked as they turned back towards home.

Finley's face scrunched up. "Not really. The palace is pretty far back in the stone age when it comes to technology."

Malcolm laughed. "I guess I can see that. We don't do much on the computer, but we should probably get it fixed."

The younger man rubbed his forehead. "Yes, you should definitely put it on some priority list. I've been bugging Adrian about this for years. He keeps telling me it'll get done, but it's never high enough priority to actually *get* done."

With a grunt, Malcolm agreed. "Probably because it'd have to be approved by our parents. Things may be easier now." A burning in his gut flashed through him at the thought of his pa. He'd been trying *not* to think about his loss, but the sadness came out of nowhere.

The conversation dropped away again. It wasn't an awkward silence; the two just stopped talking and enjoyed the ride. Eventually, as Malcolm's pain ebbed, he sought for something to distract him from thinking about his pa. "So, tell me. You seem so pleasant now. For all those years, you always played those pranks on me…why not anyone else?"

Finley shrugged, a blush coloring his cheeks. "I was a kid; who knows the way of a kid's mind?"

Malcolm shot the younger man a glance, but he didn't look like he wanted to say more. He wasn't sure what Finley was hiding, or if it even mattered. He decided he'd prefer to keep things as they were and not pry. As the horses clomped down the path—despite his decision—Malcolm continued to watch Finley out of the corner of his eye, considering him.

CHAPTER 5

The water flowed over Finley, cool and refreshing on the unseasonably warm day. He'd been swimming for almost an hour. He and Adrian had decided to spend the afternoon in the pool while Anastasia and Malcolm gallivanted around in America trying to find this Jamie person everyone was all a-titter over. He didn't know much about the situation but thought it lovely that Anastasia may find this man who she apparently loved as a girl. If they still had a connection, more power to them.

When his muscles started to scream in defeat, Finley swam one last lap before giving up and moving to the hot tub—beside which sat a table which contained drinks and sweet treats. He began with the water, letting the heat relax him for maybe the first time in days. Despite the King not being his father, he'd always been more like his parent than either of his own. He'd always supported Finley and believed in him. He felt like a piece of his heart was gone forever.

Ever since his ride with Malcolm, the first time the two of them had ever spoken civilly, he'd been on edge. As long as he knew the pompous Prince despised him—or at least saw him as less than worthy—his life had been simple. He could pine for Adrian's older brother without worry of being found out.

Over the last few days, Adrian's older brother had been treating Finley like a person, and he didn't know how to handle it. His instinct had been to hide or play a prank on the man to put things back to rights and rebuild the wall between them. But during the grieving of his father wasn't the right time to do either.

Adrian finally joined him, sighing in apparent pleasure at the heat the hot tub provided.

They sat for a few minutes before Finley asked, "How long do you think they'll be gone?"

Adrian's head rested back, and his eyes were closed. "Why, Fin, you miss my siblings already? If I didn't know better, I'd think you were hoping to pick a fight with one of them."

Finley rubbed his face. "Nah, I'm just curious about what 's going on. It's so mysterious; a ring left in America all these years, Anastasia rushing off to find true love." He clasped his hands over his heart. "Such love. It almost warms the cold rock in my chest."

Adrian sat up giving him a shocked look. "Say it isn't so, Fin. Not you. You've always been standoffish with the ladies. Don't tell me this…*this* will be the thing that melts the iceberg that is your heart."

With a laugh, Finley sank deeper into the hot water. "Nah, don't worry. I'm still cold through and through."

"I worry about you, you know." His friend's eyes narrowed. "In all the time I've known you, you've never been in a serious relationship, not even when we were in college. I don't even remember you going on any dates… have you dated since?"

Finley's head fell back, and he had to work at not sinking under the too-hot liquid. He'd had these conversations with his other friends but had avoided them with Adrian…until now. He was pretty sure Adrian wouldn't care, but as a child his family had made their opinions clear, and in his youth, he'd lost some friends who'd suspected. He'd decided then he wouldn't tell anyone. It was years and a lifetime later, but he couldn't make himself abandon his decision or break his promise to himself.

Well, it was his fault; he'd sort of started this idiocy.

"I've dated…just nothing long term, like your debacle of a girlfriend sophomore and junior year of college. I've just… I've just been more discrete."

A low grumble came from Adrian. "But I'm like a brother to you, I should know these things."

"Maybe, but some things people like to keep secret. You know, not tell because of the reaction of the people around them."

Adrian tilted his head. "Are you talking about me or your parents?"

"Mostly my parents. They're a bit like Sidney…and you know that. Not the easiest to explain things to. Stuck in the past."

All the color drained from Adrian's face. "Well, darn it all; that explains so much!"

Finley felt like he'd missed half the conversation, though he had been the one trying to explain things.

Adrian leapt from the tub, grabbing a towel and quickly drying off. "Well, come on now; we need to figure this out!"

Did I hit a wall and pass out for a spell? Did half the conversation happen while I was asleep? What the bloody hell is he going on about?

Gazing at him, Adrian's face darkened. "Don't just sit there with your mouth half-opened, I'll explain on the way."

With a sigh, Finley lifted himself from the water, dried off, and slipped on a pair of cargo shorts, a shirt, and shoes.

Adrian led him down the main hall. "I think this Jamie person Anastasia is tracking down is actually a lady, not a man. And if that's the case, we're all in a bit of a pickle. There's a law, old and antiquated, but it's in the books. I remember reading it years ago…Fin, I think Anastasia may be on a fool's errand."

CHAPTER 6

Malcolm enjoyed going to the club. The trip to America had been a success, and they'd convinced Jamie to return to Ixica with them. After a few stressful days learning that the law may or may not be on their side, he decided Anastasia and Jamie needed a night out, and what better way to blow off steam than dancing at the club? There was more than one in Fridon, but only one had been cleared by security.

Though the security detail was around, he'd decided to stay close to his sister and Jamie just in case. No one knew Jamie was Anastasia's prospective bride, but leaks happened, and having extra people around was never a bad thing, especially with the drinks he'd ordered up. Jamie started to wobble after the first sip, though it hadn't stopped her from going back for more. The deal they had with the bartender assured the drinks stayed full. He would've felt bad, but they were having too much fun.

Jamie swung her hands in the air, spinning between him and Anastasia. "I haven't felt this free in…God…I don't know."

She placed her hands on his shoulders and they swayed to the music. With a wink, Anastasia headed to the table to rest for a minute and get something to drink. He leaned down. "Having fun?"

Jamie's eyes danced. "Yes! Though, I was aiming for Star. Where did she go?" Malcolm smiled at Anastasia's childhood nickname. Despite years separating her from the moniker, Jamie seemed stuck on it. He loved hearing her say it as well; it seemed to bring the two closer together.

"To the table for a breather. No worries, we're all just having fun tonight."

Out of the corner of his eyes, he saw Adrian reach the table with Finley. On the one hand, he liked the idea of more of them there to watch over Jamie. She really had no idea what she was doing in Ixica. On the other hand, he couldn't believe what Adrian and his friend considered club clothes; it baffled him. Maybe straight women didn't care about clothes as much as gay men did? At least he made sure Anastasia and Jamie came in club appropriate attire.

He leaned down to be heard. "Let's go get something to drink." After her nod, he led Jamie to the table. He liked this spunky American and hoped it worked out for her and his sister. The two made a great match.

"And then the whole thing crashed! It was bonkers." Finley finished telling an animated story to Anastasia who laughed and clapped her hands.

She shook her head. "That's crazy. Your job sounds boring on paper, but to hear you tell it, it's fantastic!"

He blushed. "Well, in reality it is rather dull, but I love it." Finley turned and spied the two of them and shook his head. "Well, we're here to dance." He spun on his heel and disappeared into the crowd. Malcolm watched him, knowing he wouldn't be alone long; ugly clothes or not, he was known to be associated with the royal family.

For a moment, Malcolm wondered about Finley's job, a bit curious about the stories, but then the thought was lost in the haze of music, alcohol, and lights. He winked at Anastasia. "Your lady friend may need a moment."

"I do not." Jamie punched his arm. "You dragged me off the dance floor, not the other way around. I think you're pooped." She pointed her thumb towards Finley. "How long have you known him anyway? It seems odd; he isn't from Ixica, is he?"

After draining his glass, Adrian hooked his arm in hers. "Nah, he and I go back to before I even met you. We went to camp together, then he and I figured out ways to terrorize anyone and everyone we could—especially Malcolm. Come on, let's go find him and dance! These two are real sticks in the mud."

She threw her head back and laughed, letting herself be dragged out to the dancefloor.

Anastasia's eyes narrowed. "That's either going to end well, or horribly."

Tilting his glass to her, Malcolm smiled mischievously. "Oh, sis, with those three, there is only one way that will end." And after a drink, he followed the troublemakers out to dance.

CHAPTER 7

Finley danced with everyone and enjoyed the night. He'd just met Jamie, but she seemed brilliant. He was excited about Anastasia finally finding someone to love. The two of them seemed so perfectly matched. He'd known for years that she preferred women and had hidden the fact from her parents. Having done the same, he'd felt they were kindred spirit. He just knew he'd never experience the same freedom of telling his parents the truth.

The five of them danced. People from town would join them, and he, Adrian, or Malcolm would break off for a song or two and then return. Everyone at the club knew who they were and one of the big things the royal family prided themselves on was they wanted to be part of the community. If they were at the club dancing, they wouldn't snub other dancers.

During one of the breaks, Anastasia and Jamie headed out. He watched them leave, a bit sad. Having them there provided a buffer between him and Malcolm, but also kept Malcolm nearby. Disappointment spiked through him when he could no longer see them, knowing their group was about to break up. The women were gone, and the three men were on their own.

As he'd predicted, Malcolm sauntered up to a man in the back of the bar wearing similar clothes to him: tight pants and a tighter top. Just seeing Malcolm made Finley's heart pound faster. When the stranger and Malcolm started dancing together, Finley was glad his own pants were loose. Things would've been very uncomfortable otherwise. The two men were beautiful.

With a groan, he forced himself to turn away. Adrian had been saying something, but he'd missed it. With a half-smile, Finley cocked his head towards the dance floor. "Shall we?"

They headed out and with the speed of a gorgeous royal, Adrian had several women swarming them. Jaw locked, and remembering he loved to dance, Finley lost himself in the music, ignoring the blond woman trying to mold her body to his. It wasn't like the dance floor was going to lead to anything more.

A second woman came up to dance behind him and he tensed. Closing his eyes, he let the music seep into him again, ignoring the people around him. It guided his body, regardless of the people dancing with him. He was here to support Adrian, not here to find someone to take home. The only person he really wanted to go home with would be returning to the palace with him, just going to a different room…always a different room.

Adrian's voice floated over the crowd next to him, laughing in delight. With slow calming breaths, he let the current song finish, then slowly made his way back to the table. As always, the glasses were refilled, and he quickly downed his sweet drink.

The room began to swim, so he sat, knowing if he tried to dance, or walk, he may fall over. From where he sat, he could see Malcolm with the other beautiful man. Sweat broke out on Finley's back and his heart pounded faster. He knew he shouldn't watch, but try as he might, he couldn't look away. He wished he were alone and could drop his hand into his lap, but too many people around could see him.

Why can't I just go over to some bloke and ask him to dance? What the fuck am I so damned worried about?

All his life, that had been the question, but the answer was one he wasn't ready to face.

CHAPTER 8

King. They wanted him to be king.

Sidney sat him down in the family's formal living room. "Your sister has decided to abdicate the throne…for love." His voice dripped with scorn.

"You had to know this was coming, Sidney; she's been saying it for days. But why me?" It felt like his blood had been transformed into ice cold water. He fought to stop the trembling.

Mom's voice, a warm breeze on a cool day. "You are our son, our second born, and you'll do great, Malcolm."

He wasn't as sure as they were, but he bit his tongue. He'd learned enough from years of training to do that much.

Malcolm still couldn't believe it. And then, to make matters worse, he was being held prisoner in the palace. After years of not paying attention, he had to learn how to be King. He didn't have much time to make up for all the lessons lost.

It was too much. Malcolm slammed out of his room to the pool for a swim. Maybe laps would take the edge off his anger. He'd already endured two hours with Sidney that morning, and the man expected another hour and a half before supper. It just may kill him…or at least, one of them.

Before he headed down the stairs, Malcolm looked out over the sunroom to the outdoors, hoping the view would help to cool him down. His hope for peace was shattered when he spotted Finley sitting in the hot tub, head leaning back, eyes closed. He looked like he was trying to relax, but that wasn't the point. Malcolm didn't want him there.

With a small sound of disgust, he headed down the stairs anyway. Maybe Finley would get tired and leave while Malcolm swam. Exiting the sunroom, he prepared to dive into the pool, but a stiff wind sent chills down his spine. *Bloody hell, it's freezing out here today. Much too cold to swim. Damn it all to hell. Do I suck it up and swim, go back inside and give up my time out here, or face the hot tub with* him?

Malcolm stood there, glowering, for several seconds before Finley grunted. He leaned back with his eyes closed. "If you want me to leave, I will, Your Highness. It *is* your property after all." He didn't sound angry, or ironic, just resigned, as if this was his lot in life, and over the years he'd come to accept it.

Sighing, Malcolm kicked off his shoes, and tossed his shirt aside. *What the hell; maybe the company will be good for me. The ride through the woods with him wasn't awful.*

He slid into the hot water across from Finley, whose dark, wavy auburn hair looked straight and almost black from the water. His eyes were still closed, and he hadn't moved. Once Malcolm was settled, the man sighed and said, "Thank you."

"You sound as stressed as me."

Finley opened his eyes but continued to stare up at the clear blue sky. "Probably not." He paused as if debating, then sighed. "My stress is a bit of my job and a lot of me just putting it on myself...me being an idiot. You, on the other hand, have been told to change your life from something you are amazing at and love to something you don't love and will be stuck doing for quite some time. I can't imagine."

Malcolm warmed at the validation of his frustrations. Then a bit of shock went through him at how well Finley knew him. Needing to release his irritations, he thought perhaps Finley would listen while he vented some of his pent-up frustrations. "There's more. I think Jamie left because she overheard me and Anastasia arguing. Now

I'm not allowed on this rescue mission as Anastasia goes to re-woo the Lady Jamie. To top it all off, Jordan, that stable hand who brought us the horses on the day of the funeral…well, he and I had a big fight. I knew it wouldn't last—especially now that I'm going to be King—but he was my first long term relationship."

"At least you've had one." Finley's voice had been low, a mumble really, and Malcolm was pretty sure he hadn't been meant to hear it. It occurred to Malcolm again that although he'd been acquainted with Finley for over ten years, the man was a virtual stranger to him.

He stared at him. By God, Finley was attractive. He was fit and taller than him. He was pretty sure women liked tall men; *he* liked tall men.

The auburn hair and green eyes were a nice combination. When Finley wasn't being rude and mischievous, he seemed rather enjoyable to be around. Everyone else in the family liked his company—which begged the question: who was the real Finley?

Well, he was going to be King, stuck in the palace. Adrian would one day be his main advisor, also living in the palace. Finley was Adrian's best friend and would continue to visit. *I guess it's time to put the past behind us and figure out who this person is.*

Deciding Jordan was as good an opening as any, Malcolm asked, "So, you know about my dating habits.

What about you? Anyone special in your life?"

Finley's face immediately burned a bright red, matching his hair nicely. It was cute how easily the man blushed. He squeezed his eyes shut and swallowed hard, as if trying to figure out a way to answer an open-ended question, and not just something simple about dating. He finally met Malcolm's gaze for a moment before quickly looking away. "Yeah, sure, I have someone back home. Real serious."

The lie was so obvious that Malcolm was sure Finley hoped he'd just move on to another topic. He'd learn that Malcolm could be just as much a trickster as he'd been, all those years ago. "Tell me about her."

The cherry red color drained from his face as his mouth opened and closed. "Ah…she…right. Black hair…I mean, blond hair, and…" He shook his head as if trying to clear away any image that was there. Something clouding the lie he wanted to create. He slumped, sinking down to his shoulders. "There isn't anyone. Never has been. I had a few one-night stands or maybe two-night stands with some…" He closed his eyes and his voice got low. "With some guys in college, but nothing before or after that."

Malcolm's interest spiked. He straightened his spine until he loomed over the other man. "Why in bloody hell are you embarrassed? I'm telling you about splitting with my boyfriend of several years."

His green eyes, looking sad and lost, shifted up to

Malcolm as he sat tall above him. Malcolm suddenly realized how imposing he might appear but didn't really care.

Finley's voice came out soft. "There are several reasons…and you wouldn't understand them." With that, he stood, climbed out of the water, and quickly grabbed a towel to wrap around his waist. He picked up his clothes and headed into the sunroom to dry off, leaving Malcolm alone with his questions.

CHAPTER 9

Finley lay in bed, lamenting saying anything to Malcolm. Why didn't I just leave when I saw him come out to the pool area? I'm sure he didn't really want me there. We're not going to become friends one day, and this chipping away at the wall I so carefully built isn't helping.

He tried to think back to the moment his crush on Adrian's older brother started. The two were so similar in looks, yet, to Finley, they were worlds apart. When his crush started, he didn't even know Malcolm liked men, he only knew Malcolm had his heart.

He needed to do something to restore the distance

between them, but he couldn't play his usual tricks while the family was in mourning.

He wanted to leave, but he couldn't, not without saying goodbye to Adrian, who was off in Chicago. A few more days to avoid the soon-to-be-king. He'd almost told him everything in the hot tub. How susceptible he was to the man! Avoiding him really was the best option.

As the sun tried to break through the curtains he'd shut, Finley thought about the amount of time he'd spent locked in his room, hiding away since fleeing the hot tub the day before. Since he hadn't admitted his life-long crush, perhaps facing Malcolm and the family could still be in the cards. Isolating himself like this was disrespectful to the Queen.

He forced himself from bed, pulled on clean clothes, and headed down to the family dining room where he knew the Queen would be breaking her fast. If he was honest, seeing her would be a balm; she'd always been a better mother to him than his biological mum. Maybe if he was lucky, she'd be the only one up this early.

The halls were quiet as he made his way down the stairs and through the wide corridor. Not hearing any voices, he relaxed with the hope that the dining room would be empty. But, as he entered the room, two sets of eyes lifted to meet his. Malcolm, and, of course, the Queen. They seemed to be enjoying their breakfast.

He bowed his head towards her. "Good morning,

Your Majesty."

She gave a small smile. "We missed you last night at dinner. I was informed you ate in your rooms. Is everything alright?"

With an effort, he kept his focus on her. "Yes. I was waiting on word from a job and decided I would be poor company. I apologize for any ill-behavior on my part. It'll not happen again." He sat and was rewarded with a plate of waffles and sausage, and a steaming mug of coffee.

A small laugh erupted from her. "Oh, Fin, you're welcome to dine in your room if you need to finish your work. You know that. We consider you as family, not only a guest. Now, tell me about your current doings. Any security wall you can't sneak your way past?"

From the corner of his eye, he saw Malcolm's brows dip in confusion. Perhaps Malcolm believed his mum didn't know what Finley did for a living. As he finished his waffles and first mug of coffee, he explained his current job and how if he'd been stymied by someone's firewall, he wouldn't *have* an independent consulting job anymore.

Once he was done, she gave him a winning smile. "Wonderful. I hope your parents are finally as proud of you as I am." At the mention of his parents, he couldn't stop his shoulders from drooping. He tried, but it was, as always, a sore spot. They were disappointed in him for not becoming a lawyer and continuing the family legacy. Sharks, every last one of them.

She patted his arm. "I'm sorry, son. I know how hard it's been over the years with their continual disapproval. I hoped they'd finally seen what amazing things you've accomplished."

Finley nodded, wishing this discussion wasn't happening in front of Malcolm. He'd cried to Adrian's parents when he was young about parents who didn't love him. And then again, when he was older, and they refused to come to his graduation. The King and Queen of Ixica came, but his parents hadn't because he'd graduated with a degree in IT, and not a law degree.

"You know, I think you need to get out of that room. And maybe out of your head…just like when you were younger. I've heard through the grapevine that Anastasia and Adrian may be bringing Jamie back tomorrow with a few of her friends. I know you don't do a lot in that guest living room, but why don't you and Malcolm give it a quick dusting and a once over."

Malcolm gaped at her. "What? Don't we have people to do that?"

She winked at Finley before turning to her son. "Would you rather spend the morning with Sidney? Learning humility *is* part of learning to be a good King."

He sighed and faced Finley. "Well, what do you say? A day of cleaning, then?"

Finley's insides churned at the thought of an entire day

spent with Malcolm in a small room. Well, not that small, but small enough. The two of them working together…and possibly talking. But the Queen had spoken; what was he going to do? "Sounds delightful, mate. Lead on."

With his stomach in knots, Finley followed Malcolm, trying not to stare at the man ahead of him. *Would he feel my eyes on him, trying to drink in every inch of his body? Memorize him for later since this will never happen again?*

The room didn't need much cleaning. Waiting in the center of the room was a cart with cleaning supplies the staff must have left for them. When Finley didn't live here, his life was mundane, so he knew how to clean. He grabbed a rag and started to dust the shelves from the highest he could reach. He heard Malcolm sweeping, and Finley groaned.

He let his arms drop as he turned to see Malcolm with a broom, starting in the center of the room. "Your Highness, what are you doing?"

Malcolm straightened, leaning on the broom. "Well, in case you don't know what this is, it's called a broom. It is used to clean the floor of an abode like this." His voice dripped with a derogatory tone as he mimed sweeping without having the bristles actually touch the ground.

Finley dropped onto one of the couches and stared into Malcolm's jewel-like blue eyes as he got mocked. "Well, Your Highness." He bowed his head a bit and saw the slight tightening of Malcolm's jaw at the words. "I, unlike you, have used one of those contraptions. When I'm not here, I don't actually live with servants, if you didn't know. At home, I'm usually the one who does the cleaning. If you sweep first, then once I'm done dusting the shelves, you, or probably me…I'll have to sweep again." He wiggled his fingers imitating rain. "All the dust floats down, then you sweep."

He quickly stood before his insides tightened anymore. He wasn't sure how much longer he could be in a room with Malcolm. Maybe Malcolm would get fed up and leave. Then Finley would just clean the bloody room himself.

He snatched a jar from one of the shelves and vaguely heard Malcolm's voice from behind him laughingly say, "Hey, I remember those from way back." As he wiped the jar, the top flipped open.

A wailing from the depths of hell came echoing out from the canister, a scream to wake the dead. Worse, the battery in the vessel was dying, and the sound could've been from the basement of a horror movie as a demon scraped its way up the stairs…slowly.

Finley held the canister, thinking back fourteen years to when he and Adrian first rediscovered the jars.

He turned to his friend. "These are amazing. Can we re-record the sound the jar makes?"

Adrian's face scrunched up. "I guess. I mean, no one uses the jars. Sure, it won't matter."

They'd gathered the three vessels and headed out to the back part of the grounds and practiced different sounds. They'd given each canister a different scream. One was delight, one surprise, and the one Finley currently held…agony.

As the sound wound down and finally ended, he opened his eyes to see the room filled with servants and security, all wide-eyed and searching for the dying demon from hell. Being stabbed would've been less painful. He took two steps and handed the vessel to the first person he came to, and then hurried from the living room. He slipped into his own room down the hall. He'd had enough of this day…maybe enough of this 'royal' life.

CHAPTER 10

Malcolm stared at the servant holding the vessel and began to laugh. He took the offending object from her and placed it on the table. "I think we're fine in here; you lot can be off. Back to your duties. We're all safe from the scary treat jar of doom."

The people who'd come to save him and Finley chuckled as they turned to leave. Checking out the room, not yet clean, but better than it had been, Malcolm wanted to find out how the other jars' messages had been altered, probably due to Finley's own ministrations, but didn't want to bring the palace staff down on this room again. He'd save that for another day.

"Well, I'd better see where my partner in crime went off to." Three weren't many other likely places on this floor, but Malcolm's eyes fell on the door to Finley's suite. Everyone knew which rooms were his. It had been a guest suite for about the first three years of his visiting, but then it just sort of shifted and became Finley's. No one used it but him.

He thought about knocking, but he'd never knocked on Adrian or Anastasia's doors; why start now? He passed through the sitting room. Looking around, he noticed Finley had a small bookcase lined with books. With a raised eyebrow of interest, he continued to the bedroom.

Finley lay on his back with his arm covering his face. In the corner was the most elaborate computer setup Malcolm had ever seen. Three monitors, all chugging over something, with data flowing on screens faster than he could make out, even if he were to pay attention. There were even two keyboards. Never in a million years could he even begin to understand it all. He had to pull his focus away and remember why he'd come in.

Leaning on the doorframe between rooms, he asked, "You okay?"

Finley's body stiffened. He acknowledged Malcolm's question with a grunt.

Malcolm shook his head and walked over to sit on the edge of the bed. From this close, he could see Finley's clenched jaw. He tried to think of something to say, but Finley beat him to it. "I'm sorry about that." His voice was soft and tight. "It was from one of my first summers here. Honestly, I'd forgotten about it."

Malcolm put his hand on Finley's shin to soothe him, but it had the opposite effect. The man tensed more, if that was possible, and took in a sharp gulp of air. Malcolm laughed and said, "No worries, it was rather funny, really. I like seeing you get punked by one of your own pranks. Made my day."

At last, Finley seemed to relax, and his arm slid over his head. He chuckled. After a moment of looking at Malcolm, he propped himself on his elbows, getting closer to eye level. "I wasn't that bad, you know. I never did that many pranks. You're exaggerating my prowess. A few each summer, that's it."

Eyebrow popping up to new levels, Malcolm shook his head in disbelief. "Yes, you were. For years you were awful."

Finley opened his mouth as if to argue or make a point, but then closed it and shook his head. Opening his mouth, he took a large breath. As if wanting to clear the air, he said, "We should probably get back, maybe destroy those jars before someone else gets a nice surprise…especially with the batteries dying."

He started to rise, but Malcolm put a hand on his chest to stop him. Finley immediately stopped moving, his eyes as wide as saucers. "Are you ready to tell me why I've always been the target of all your pranks?" His curiosity was piqued and he hoped he would finally learn the truth.

Finley's eyes darkened to the green of the trees in a deep forest. His voice came out thready and low. "Dumb luck, I guess."

It suddenly occurred to Malcolm that he was sitting in bed with Finley, unchaperoned. Standing, he offered his hand to help the other man up. "Right. Back to cleaning?"

With a groan, Finley dropped back down to his pillow. "Give me a minute, if you would. I'll be right behind you."

Malcolm rolled his eyes as he headed out, figuring he wouldn't see of the scamp who'd terrorized him for years again that day.

CHAPTER 11

As the door clicked shut, Finley began to shake. *Was Malcolm really in my room, sitting on my bed? Did he put his hand on my chest?*

Finley knew he should return to help with the guest living room, but he needed a moment to compose himself. Everything that Malcolm had done had been innocent, but his body didn't seem to understand that.

He tried to get his heart to slow, but he could still feel the heat from Malcolm's hand on his body and it made him tremble more to think about it. *I must get a handle on myself and these wild emotions! Force myself to relax.* Finley tried to clear his mind of anything relating to Malcolm.

A few deep breaths later, he sat up and knew he'd taken more time than he should. He wished he had more, but that wasn't in the cards. If he survived today, then Adrian would be back tomorrow. Finley could go home to London and put this whole affair behind him. It was earlier than planned, but he knew his limits, and he was already past them.

When he finally made it back to the guest living room, he shot Malcolm a quick look to see the broom back in his hand, before Finley focused on the shelves. Malcolm jerked in apparent shock when he noticed him dusting shelves on the other side of the room. "You did return!"

"Of course, I did," he mumbled low to the shelf. *Why does the arrogant Prince think I would avoid this responsibility? Is it because he would?* He rolled his eyes at how little Malcolm knew him.

Finley finished dusting the jars and put them up on the high shelf. Malcolm's comment told him everything he needed to know about their moment of civility. It had been a fluke and was very much over. He finished up the last shelf and searched the cart for a small vacuum to use on the back of the couch.

Turning, he bumped into Malcolm, who was back to sweeping. He watched the soon-to-be-king drag the bristles across the floor and Finley knew he was done with all of it. "Why don't you go do your playboy things…I'll clean up the room, Your Highness." He bowed low. It was awkward with the mini-vacuum in his hand. He fought to stop his face from showing any emotion, his body trembling. He seethed with his own turbulent emotions. All he wanted right then was to be alone. The act of cleaning would help to dispel some of his turmoil.

Malcolm's brows came together, and his head tilted. "What? Am I doing this wrong?" He searched the floor as if trying to find where he'd made a mistake.

Finley's nails dug into his palms as he looked Malcolm up and down, trying to figure out how to say the words he needed without giving his emotions away, then he turned to do a survey of the room himself. "As I mentioned before, it's better to start high and leave the floor for the very end, your Majesty. You're sweeping again. But who am I to critique the future King?" He bowed low, as Adrian had taught him. Lifting back up, he spun on his heel and moved to the tables and lower shelves on the other side of the room.

His hands were shaking as he lifted his rag and continued to work. The vacuuming could wait. As he lifted each item to dust under it, he refused to check if Malcolm was in the room. He didn't hear the future King but didn't want to look for the man. If he were still there, he'd see how much he affected him, and Finley couldn't expose himself more than he had. Anger burned through his veins, and it forced him to focus and not break any item as he continued to systematically dust across the back of the room.

Why can't I get over him? I've spent most of my life pining over someone who doesn't see me as anything other than a nuisance. If I could get past the future King, maybe I could do as Adrian demanded, and find someone. But would anyone make my heart stop like Malcolm does?

Once he completed the dusting, he placed both his hands on the last table and just breathed. He could feel his muscles still straining with the stress of the day, and all he wanted to do was scream. Biting his cheek, he straightened to go get the twice damned broom. With a huff, he turned and crashed into Malcolm.

With a shock, he put up his hands, stepping back and tripping, almost falling over. Malcolm's hand shot out and he caught Finley, locking him into the small space between the table and the soon to be King. Finley stammered out, "Excuse me."

With a quirk of his mouth, Malcolm said, "No."

Finley nodded and went to move past Malcolm when his mind caught up with the answer. "Wait, what?"

Malcolm still held his arm. His brow rose in challenge. "I don't think I will excuse you."

Finley wondered if Malcolm could feel his pulse beating as his heart sped up. Shivers raced up and down his spine and he started to tremble, unable to control it this close to Malcolm. "Excuse me, please. I can't clean with you holding me." He hated how weak and breathy his voice sounded.

The pressure on his arm tightened a bit. "What, no 'Your Highness' this time?" Finley could hear the laughter in Malcolm's voice; he was playing with him.

His voice almost a whisper, Finley tried to maintain eye contact. "Is that what you want?"

Malcolm's smile tightened and his light, joking air turned into a hard glare. Finley tried to focus on Malcolm's face and whatever he'd say next, but the sensation of Malcolm's hands on his arms distracted him. With a sudden jerk, Malcolm pulled him in, and their chests came together. Malcolm reached up to cup Finley's face, pulling him down for a kiss.

Stunned, Finley's brain short-circuited. Before he knew what was happening, his body leaned in and his tongue probed out, deepening the kiss. He was rewarded as he got a taste of this frustrating dream man. Heat pooled in his groin as all the irritations of his day with Malcolm built within him and he groaned.

Suddenly, Malcolm stepped back, hands dropping away, a look of disgust and horror on his face. The future King shook his head with a sneer, spun on his heel, and stalked from the room.

Breathing hard, Finley closed his eyes and gave his body time to calm down. With a shake of his head, he went to collect the broom to finish cleaning the room, biting back the tears that threatened to fall.

CHAPTER 12

Malcolm's muscles burned as he swam lap after lap. He knew he shouldn't have left Finley to finish cleaning that awful room, but he was pretty sure they were close to done. He may not be as adept as the other man at cleaning, but the room had felt cleaner. Then again, his mother *had* sent both of them to do the cleaning and by all accounts Finley *was* a guest. Guests shouldn't be cleaning.

Yeah, right, a guest. Finley hadn't been a guest in years. Calling that man a guest was a joke. But Malcolm couldn't go back; he had to get away from him, he was driving him crazy. *If he drives you crazy, King boy, why did you kiss him?*

We were cleaning the room, he kept bowing and then…God above, he just pissed me off. Then he was in my arms. It felt good. I kept thinking what if we did more…but no! I will not admit that again, not even to myself. What am I thinking! Finley is Adrian's friend; a trickster, not someone to kiss.

He upped his speed; fire burned in his muscles as he swam. He'd erase the memory of the kiss from his mind, his lips, his soul, even if it killed him. That kiss. He'd kissed other men, he'd been with Jordan for years, but nothing had zinged through his body. What more could zing…*No! Stop thinking about it—about him! He's the same annoying kid he's always been.*

He swam another lap, mind going numb with the rhythm of his strokes. *I just want things to go back, back to the way it was before…before that soul-shattering kiss which could lead to…no! Stop thinking about it, reliving it.*

Finley will go home soon…or, maybe he'll want to play one more time. Maybe that will get the man out of my system and I can go back to living my life. God above, Malcolm, keep it in your pants! Despite his self-admonition, he kept contemplating scenarios as he swam, trying to determine if that was a genius idea, or the stupidest one he'd had in ages.

As he reached the wall and was about to turn, he heard his name. Standing, he faced the house and saw the man he'd been ruminating over. He stood halfway between the house and the pool, shoulders stooped, face drawn. Had he been watching him? Hardening his own face, Malcolm snapped, "What do you want?"

Finley slouched as if he'd been knocked down. Looking closer, his eyes seemed sad, and he was clenching his jaw again. He didn't appear to want to be out there. He seemed more like a kicked dog than a voyeur.

Finley licked his lips and said, "When I left the guest living room, I ran into Sidney. I explained you were only gone for a minute, but he followed me to my next spot and waited. When you didn't immediately return, he told me to find you. He said, if you were free, he had a lesson for you." Message delivered, Finley gave a small bow and spun to leave.

Scrunching up his face at the idea of an afternoon with Sidney, Malcolm raised his hand, but realized Finley's back was to him. "Is there more cleaning to do?"

Finley froze at the door, his back to Malcolm. Malcolm tried not to notice how good he looked from behind. *What has gotten into me? I've known the kid for over ten years, and now this? Kid? He's a year younger than me, a year older than Adrian…not so much a kid, and not bad looking—coming or going.*

Resting his hands on the glass, Finley sighed. "I thought I would check out the two main guest rooms across from mine. I figure, after all these years, I know what should be in them as well as anyone else on staff. If that's all, I'll be leaving now."

Malcolm walked to the side of the pool and climbed out. "I'm going to help you."

Almost perfectly mimicking what Malcolm had done earlier, Finley said, "No." Unlike him, after a beat in which Malcolm dried off, Finley continued, "Please don't."

Coming to stand behind him, Malcolm asked quietly, "Why?" He knew he'd handled the last room poorly, but was there more to it than that? Had he offended the man? Scared him off? He'd mentioned dating men, so the kiss couldn't have been that horrible.

Finley adjusted so he rested his head on his arm, his whole body tense. After a few seconds, Malcolm wondered if he'd answer as he finished drying and pulled on his clothes. But then Finley finally began speaking. "What just happened up in the room, between us, to you, it was nothing, a game. I just…I need time away from you to remind myself that you don't like me, then I can more easily keep my distance, okay?"

The words shocked Malcolm. Years of interaction with the other man started to fall into place and make sense. He replayed their relationship and interactions from Finley's point of view, a younger man with a crush on someone that he felt would never go anywhere. How would he deal with it…force the distance?

Heart breaking for a man who'd been hurting for all

these years, he reached out and placed his hand on Finley's shoulder. Finley shivered at the contact, and it occurred to him that that had happened every time they'd touched during the day. He wished he could help soothe the pain in the other man. "I'm sorry."

Finley shook his head. "I'd be easier if we didn't… anything." And before Malcolm could do or say anything else, Finley slipped through the door and left.

CHAPTER 13

Finley sat in a chair, elbows on knees, holding his head. He'd come into the guest room across from his, a mirror of his own room, with the plan to get it set up. As soon as he'd finished circling the room, he realized he needed to decompress. He'd finally done it. Malcolm knew.

You did it, Fin, for better or worse, the future King knows. Now maybe he'll leave you alone. You can lick your wounds and move on with your life. Clean this room, maybe take dinner in my room, then see Adrian tomorrow before returning to London. Enough of this place. It is time to focus on anything but Malcolm.

His initial circuit of the room showed him it had all the basic necessities. The servants had done a good job and he didn't see anything more he could do. He was pretty sure he was free and clear and done with palace duties.

He decided it was time to shower and get ready for dinner. He had no real excuse to skip again tonight, no matter how much he may want to. With a grunt, he stood and crossed the hall.

As he entered his room and shut the door, he debated locking it. Last time Malcolm had just walked in, but he figured he didn't have to worry about that again. He'd never locked his door before, and he wasn't going to start being paranoid now.

He stripped off his clothes and threw them in the hamper of his walk-in closet. Dinner with the Queen meant nice clothes, so he flipped through options until he found something appropriate for the evening. Most of his trousers were cargo, but he found a pair of black slacks and a charcoal button-down shirt. Folding the clothes over an arm, he grabbed a pair of socks and undies from a drawer before heading back out to the main room.

Finley went to lay the outfit on his bed for after his shower but froze, the clothes covering his naked bits, and stared at Malcolm sitting on his bed...again. Though his clothes covered him, heat burned his face. He gaped at the other man lounging in his room as if he owned the place...

which…once he got his mind working again…he realized he did…or would. Gah!

Finley gulped to get moisture in his mouth. "Um…can I help you? Why are you here?"

Slowly, oh, so slowly, Malcolm's eyes traveled up and down his body. The clothes Finley held covered him more than a swimsuit, but he still felt very exposed. "Nice outfit."

He wondered if Malcolm meant the one he held or the one he wasn't wearing. Feeling his face burn hotter, he just waited, not knowing what else to do or say. *I should just go shower.*

Malcolm's head tilted as he watched Finley fidget. "Do you always saunter around your rooms naked? Because these are the things I think I should know…you know, as host, and future King."

Finley closed his eyes and tried to slow his heart. He worried about a heart attack after the day he'd had. "I was about to shower. It usually helps to be naked when showering." He tried to keep his voice steady as he spoke, but his mind whirled. *I can't believe how many times we've said 'naked'! Gah! I have to get away!*

With a sigh, Malcolm shrugged. "Oh, well. It was such an intriguing image…you in here, naked all the time. I'm just wondering why I haven't been popping in unannounced for years. It would've been a right jolly old show, especially with how red you get."

Placing his socks and undies on the table next to him, Finley rubbed his eyes in frustration. He was tired of waiting. "What are you doing here, Malcolm? How can I help you?"

Malcolm's eyes got wide. "You *do* know my name after all. I'm thrilled. Now, what I want to say can wait; go off and shower…you're welcome to leave your clothes, though." He smirked.

Finley grabbed his underclothes and walked into the washroom, knowing he flashed his backside to his 'guest.' At this point, getting away was his bigger priority…and once he was clean, he could put his clothes on; that was a priority as well.

He placed the clothes on a counter and started the double-headed shower. He didn't wait long to walk in, letting the warm water wash away the dust and grime from the day of cleaning.

A full day trying to keep his distance from the one person he didn't want to keep his distance from. It was like a dream and nightmare rolled into one…and that kiss. It was everything he'd hoped for, right up until the moment he realized he'd messed it up, and the man he'd secretly swooned over hated it. The image of Malcolm's disgust would be burned in his head forever.

Yet he still won't leave me alone. But that's because the alternative is Sidney, and he thinks I'm just barely better than him.

The shampoo smelled of coconut and the soap of peppermint. Once he'd gotten everything scrubbed, he placed his hands on the walls of the large area and let the water beat on him, finally starting to breathe freely and relax. He couldn't believe how stressful the day had been.

Finley wanted to bang his head against the shower wall but feared the noise may bring the man from his thoughts into the washroom and facing him nude was beyond him.

Just as he finished that thought, a pair of warm hands wrapped around his waist and his mind completely short-circuited.

CHAPTER 14

Malcolm watched Finley head into the washroom, his taut body a wonder to see. *That man covers up lovely... assets...in horrible clothes.* How many years had he ignored what was right in front of him? Of course, much of that was by Finley's own doing, but how was he so blind? Was it just him ignoring anything associated with his brother?

If he were honest with himself, he wasn't exactly sure why he was in Finley's room. He'd been heading to his own room to avoid Sidney when he saw Finley crossing the hall. He'd moved robotically, and something in Malcolm snapped. He wasn't sure why, but he wanted the old Finley back, the prankster who laughed and played. He hated to think Finley was only happy if Adrian was around. *Why can't I get him to smile?*

The next thing he knew, he'd walked into the room. He wasn't in the sitting room or main room, so Malcolm flopped on the bed and waited. He wasn't disappointed when Finley stepped from the closet.

As he thought about Finley and his blushing, Malcolm realized he'd moved to the washroom. *What am I doing?* He stood with both hands against the door and listened to the water running. His body tightened with the thought of Finley in there, wet and naked.

Breath coming fast, he acted without thought. He stripped off his clothes and quietly entered the steamy room…why not? He saw Finley standing with his hands against the wall letting the water hit him. The man was beautiful. Malcolm's body got harder staring at him. *Just get it out of your system. Give yourself this one night, and you'll be over the rascal.*

He decided to throw all caution to the wind, and he quietly entered the shower area, and, stepping up behind Finley, placed his hands on the man's hips, letting his hands slide around his taut waist, pulling him back so they were pressed together. Finley tensed, then leaned back, accepting the moment and getting more contact between them.

Malcolm's face pressed into Finley's peppermint-scented back as he held him tight. He let one hand roam up, feeling how solid the man's abs were; the other traveled south, grasping his impressively large cock, thick and warm, obviously excited about Malcolm's presence.

He began to move his hand up and down and with each stroke, Finley whimpered and groaned, the fingers of his hands trying to dig into the tiles of the shower wall. Malcolm wanted to do more, bite and suck, but the showers beat down on both of them, restricting their movements. He continued to touch and play until Finley exclaimed his pleasure, his seed mixing with the shower water.

After taking a bit of time to catch his breath, Finley finally turned to gaze at him, a fire in his green eyes. "Please tell me I get to reciprocate." His hot scrutiny trailed from Malcolm's head to his toes and back in a slow investigation. Malcolm had never felt so treasured.

"What are you thinking?"

Finley bit his lower lip before he leaned down and kissed Malcolm. The kiss was every bit as good as the first one and Malcolm slid his hands around Finley's waist, letting him deepen the kiss again. Finley's tongue traced every centimeter of Malcolm's mouth before he pulled back and moved to Malcolm's ear. "I want to taste other areas of your body, Your Highness."

For the first time, the title didn't sound like a sneer. Spinning them, so Malcolm's back was to the wall, Finley began kissing his way down Malcolm's body, ignoring the shower sprays. As he moved down, he lowered himself to his knees, before sliding Malcolm's cock into his hot mouth.

Malcolm watched Finley's movements at first, fascinated as his dick fit so nicely in this man's mouth, going deeper and deeper each stroke, but then the heat and sensations built, and he threw his head back with a moan. The man's mouth was magic; as his tongue undulated, Finley's hand slid between his legs, stimulating Malcolm's balls, and his other hand helped with the length of his cock.

As Finley continued, he slid one hand up to rub Malcolm's abs and he moaned as he investigated Malcolm's body. The added groaning put Malcolm over and he tried to grasp the tile wall as his body clenched and released.

Once Malcolm could stand on his own, Finley stood and turned off the water. He handed Malcolm a towel as he started to dry off himself. Without making eye contact, Finley went to grab his undies, but Malcolm put a hand on his arm. He tensed again, as if they hadn't just played in the shower. *Is he still nervous? I'm not going to bite…unless he wants me to bite.*

"Or…you could not put those on. We can send our regrets to my mother, say we're too tired after a day of cleaning. Your bed seems rather lovely, don't you think?"

CHAPTER 15

Finley lay on the bed. Malcolm hovered above him and asked huskily, "Where did you learn how to kiss? Because your kisses are addictive."

Am I dreaming? Did I fall and hit my head? Am I lying on a floor somewhere in need of medical attention? Hopefully someone has called for an ambulance because none of this makes any sense.

And then, he was kissing Malcolm until his toes curled. He lifted a knee, wrapped his arms around Malcolm, and sighed in bliss. He could exist like this and be satisfied… thrilled…elated for an eternity.

Malcolm broke off the kiss and trailed hot licks and nibbles down to his ear where he continued to torture him. Finley never realized how sensitive his ear could be until Malcolm's tongue and teeth began to play. Then he whispered, "Just so you know, I'm going to have my way with you tonight. Do all sorts of things to you… including fucking you."

A small whimper escaped him as Malcolm's hands rubbed down his arms to his hands. "If we were in my room, I would tie you down to make sure you couldn't stop me from doing exactly what I like, but I guess tonight we just play."

Finley could barely hear him over the blood rushing in his ears. But when Malcolm asked Finley to hold the headboard bars above his head, he slowly lifted his arms and obeyed. His mind whirled too fast to think of a reason why it may not be the best idea.

Malcolm kneeled between his legs and lifted one leg to his shoulder. "Do you have any lubrication?"

He felt his face heat as he nodded. "In my overnight bag in the bathroom."

Malcolm disappeared and returned a minute later, getting back into the same position. "I do like the toys you have in that bag; we should compare some time, maybe go shopping together."

Finley's heart did a flip at the idea that this may last

for more than one night, but then he tamped it down. Malcolm would be King. They weren't about to go to a sex shop together. He almost laughed at the idea of the King playing with the toys on display, discussing their uses, if the vibration would be enough for him, or the girth of the particular dildo. He had to stop thinking or his head may actually explode.

Malcolm rubbed lubrication on him, and—as Finley gazed down the length of his body—on himself. Then, ever so slowly, did exactly what he'd promised he'd do. He pushed himself in slower than he needed to, being extra careful. Despite the slow speed, it felt like fireworks exploded in Finley's body until their bodies came together.

He gazed down at Finley, tracing Finley's face with a finger. "Have you always been this pretty? Have I just ignored you because you were my brother's annoying friend?" He looked away, and Finley realized he gazed at the multi-computer setup. "And smart?"

It was getting to be too much. Finley smirked, finally feeling free. "Are we talking or are you going to fuck me, Your Majesty?"

Eyes lighting up, Malcolm began to pump, finding a speed that sent shimmers of electricity through Finley's body. In and out, as heat rose within him. He started to breathe harder, and his body jerked in time with Malcolm's movements. He heard Malcolm groan, getting close, too. Then, just when he was sure Malcolm was mind-numb, he grabbed Finley's cock and yanked hard in time with his pumping.

Finley watched Malcolm's muscles seize up as his body prepared to explode. He yelled out his release. "God, Finley, you better come, too; I'm not doing this alone."

Hearing his name at the time of Malcolm's release was too much, and Finley shattered, coming all over both him and Malcolm. Malcolm fell forward, catching himself before he crushed Finley. "Hmm, fancy another round in the shower? Then we can come back here and have another round on the bed. This will be fun." His eyes were a bit crazy, but insane was what Finley felt, so he did the only thing he could do, and agreed.

Finley would've followed Malcolm anywhere, and that night he did. They didn't collapse to sleep until well after three in the morning, lying together, cuddling. Though the day had been awful, the night more than made up for it.

He woke up a few hours later, knowing he should check in with work before heading down for breakfast with the Queen. Opening his eyes, it felt like a punch in the gut when he realized he was alone, and the bed was cold. Only the scent of sex in the air that told him it hadn't all been a dream. He'd had enough one-night stands to understand what just happened.

Lying there, staring at the ceiling, he wondered if it was better to have known last night was possible, a memory to treasure, or to have never known the interaction at all. Deep in his gut he felt if he could go back and skip yesterday, he'd be a much happier person. A day with Malcolm wasn't something he should've allowed to happen.

I don't know if I can process Malcolm as a one-night stand.

Though Adrian and the others would return today, if Malcolm hoped this could be something light…Finley couldn't. It would break his heart. Yesterday just proved it to him, vindicated years of his actions, let him know he'd been right to avoid the man his whole life. Why had he stopped for one day?

He sat up and leaned his head on his knees. He could stay, hiding in his room until the others returned. He had enough work…but not the good work. And he couldn't do the good work here. He *could* just pack up and go home. In the end, Adrian would understand.

As he gazed around the room—his room?—he wondered if Ixica had suddenly become less of a home to him. Less of a place that had always welcomed him. Then again, maybe he just needed space from its future King, time to find his own Prince Charming.

Having made up his mind, he got dressed in the

clothes he'd selected the night before and headed down for breakfast. He wanted to officially tell the Queen he was leaving and give his regards and gratitude for her hospitality. The family had been too kind to him over the years for him to slink away.

Once again, she wasn't eating alone. Sidney and the Queen were already there, eating. Well, it didn't matter. After being served egg in toast with a side of fresh fruit and coffee, he turned to the Queen. "Your Majesty, I wanted to thank you for allowing me time to grieve with your family. I don't want to overstay my welcome, and I have some business that requires a different caliber of firewalls. I think three guests will be enough for you to host, so I'll be heading home later today. There is a flight leaving at noon. I checked before coming down. I'll make the reservation after breakfast if that's okay."

The Queen's face tightened. "Are you sure? You know we see you as more than a guest, Fin. You are welcome to stay as long as you want."

A well of warmth burst in him, and he smiled. "Thank you, and I appreciate it. You've always been more of a family to me than my own. But yes, I'm sure. I really should head home."

She tilted her head at him. "If you wait until the others are back, you can take our plane. I know you came with a lot of luggage."

He bit his lip at her double entendre. He doubted she even knew she'd used one. "It'll be fine."

Her eyes narrowed. "I don't want to push too much, but I know your finances—and a last-minute ticket can be pricey."

He slumped. "It's the best option I could think of."

Sidney placed his silverware on his plate. "I believe the others will be arriving during the early afternoon. If you go to the airport just after lunch, our craft will get you there before the plane leaving at noon. I believe the Queen will be happier with that solution, young Master Finley."

Finley looked down and realized he'd finished his meal. He knew when he'd been outmaneuvered. He nodded his agreement. "Thank you. Then I can say goodbye to Adrian in person. If you'll excuse me, I have a lot of packing to do."

Back in his room, he was almost done packing when Malcolm walked in. "Why are you leaving?"

Numb apprehension tingled up and down his body at the sharpness in his voice. He wondered if he'd ever get over the way Malcolm affected him. "Because."

Malcolm placed a hand on Finley's arm and looked into his face. "Just tell me, no more hiding."

Turning to look down at his folded clothes, Finley shook his head. "I can't."

Malcolm pulled him away, holding his hips so they are face to face. "Just talk to me."

Finley felt the tears prickling his eyes and shifted his

gaze down and up, unable to maintain the direct eye contact. Then a tear escaped, and he gave up trying. "Because, you idiot, I love you. I always have…probably always will. I can't do this." His hand waved between them. "Casually, or alone. It will break me." He leaned down and kissed Malcolm, savoring the sweet feeling one last time. "Please leave.… I just…can't."

He turned back to securing his computer components for air flight. The door clicked behind him.

CHAPTER 16

Malcolm scooped another bite of s'mores cake into his mouth, the marshmallow and chocolate cake a balm to his frayed nerves. Anastasia and Jamie's wedding still vibrated through the halls, though the happy couple had flown to Hawaii two days ago on their honeymoon. Jamie's friends headed home the day before she'd left but agreed to come back to help Jamie transition from being an American to an Ixican Princess.

Once again, as the people in the palace scattered to all corners of the world, he was left a prisoner in his own home. Thinking back over the years, he could count on his fingers the number of times his parents had left the country. He stuffed more cake in his mouth, imagining his life boiled down to the walls of this palace. So many people who had visited were amazed at the size of the Ixican palace, but when the building was a prison, it no longer felt larger than life.

Adrian sauntered into the kitchen and headed past him towards the pantry. He disappeared, reappearing a few minutes later with a container of hot chocolate mix. Eyes settling on Malcolm, he froze. "Oh, hi. What are you doing here? Besides trying to finish off the wedding cake?"

Malcolm held up his fork. "Grab a fork while the eating's good. Why waste time with that rubbish when you can eat this?"

Adrian tilted his head, seeming to consider before he nodded. "Fair point." Adrian placed the container on the counter, dug in a drawer for a fork, and sat across from Malcolm at the table. "You've been out of sorts for several days. Care to share with the class?"

The cake felt heavy in his gut, but Malcolm dug in for another bite, not caring. "I don't know what you're talking about. I did my duty at the wedding. I wore the fancy King's robes and walked Anastasia down the aisle. I smiled and said the appropriate words. I've been doing all the extra training everyone has asked of me."

Adrian dug in, taking a chunk of cake. "That you did. You couldn't have done better at the wedding if you'd wanted to play King. But outside of being there for Anastasia, you've been snapping at everyone. The servants are drawing straws to see who goes up to your room if there's any chance you'll be around. When they see you heading for a corridor, they find a new route. And I know you and that stable hand broke up. Is that what this is all about? Because you and he couldn't have lasted with you becoming King."

Malcolm slammed down his fork and went to the stove to start a kettle for tea. "I know we are done. And no, that has nothing to do with it. Why do you suppose everything that upsets me has to do with my new job?"

His words echoed around the room. Adrian was rubbing his temples. Finally, his younger brother turned to face him. "Look, you haven't left the house in days. Why don't we go for a ride, or a walk? Just…let's get some fresh air."

Braced against the counter, Malcolm considered his last trip out of the house. If he discounted swimming in the pool, then it was when they all went out clubbing with Jamie…how long ago had that been? He reached over and turned off the kettle and nodded. "Fine. Let's go, but no horses. I really don't want to see Jordan—not right now."

They walked through the halls and out of the palace in silence, not speaking until they reached the shade of the trees. Adrian put his hand on Malcolm's arm to stop him. "Talk to me, please. Whatever is on your mind is eating you up and I don't like to see you this way."

It felt like he was being torn open and dissected. Open up to his brother? But who else was there? With a sigh, he searched the trees and the sky, trying to draw peace and tranquility from the environment. He knew once he started talking, he wouldn't find any from the subject matter. He resumed their walk. "When you went with Anastasia to collect Jamie, there was a day that me and Finley…" *What? Connected? Became friends? Had a fling?* How could he explain what had happened to not only his brother but to Finley's best friend? It was weird all around.

Adrian's mouth twitched. "You and Finley? I'm not sure where you're going with this, but I need a second to digest that one sentence."

Malcolm rubbed the bridge of his nose and debated turning around and ending this farce. "Just don't, okay? You asked and I'm trying. This is…this is difficult."

Adrian nodded. "I know, it's just…you two have never gotten along. I thought you hated him. Wait, is that why he left?" Skidding to a halt, Adrian whipped around until he stood toe to toe with Malcolm. His face hard, eyes narrow, he glared up at his older brother. "Did you alienate my best friend?"

"It wasn't what you think." Malcolm sighed, taking a step back. Thinking of the day with Finley, his shoulders dropped. "He did leave because of me…he doesn't want to be around me…he never wanted to be around me. That's why he always did what he did. To push me away."

Adrian stared at Malcolm, and Malcolm could almost see his wise brother figure things out. He was always smarter than him—maybe smarter than all of them. Adrian narrowed his eyes. "Really?"

With a groan, Malcolm admitted the rest. "Not if I won't go all in. His emotions were strained when we were forced to spend the day together, like he was about to explode."

The silence that followed was deafening. Adrian looked at him, his gaze penetrating. "Well…what do you want? Do you want to go 'all in?'"

"No! God, of course not. It's *Finley*." His answer came so fast, he wondered if either of them believed it.

Adrian nodded curtly and continued the walk. "If you're sure."

Feeling like he'd been punched in the gut…again, he caught up with his brother. His voice small, he admitted, "He's all I've thought about since he's left."

"Then go after him."

It was like someone had dunked his head in ice cold water and woken him up. "And then what?"

Adrian shrugged. "I don't know; you tell me."

CHAPTER 17

Finley slouched on his sofa, legs splayed out into the living room, flipping through the channels of his TV. He debated switching to a movie channel and vegging to something he'd seen over and over. Maybe a classic like The Matrix. If he could go and reprogram his world, would he? *Maybe leave Ixica the day Jamie headed to America. That would've made my life better, simple, drabber. As much as things suck, at least that day was a spark of color. Finley, don't pretend it wasn't.*

His eyes slid over to his computer, and he considered the last job he'd finished. It had been challenging; they'd almost caught him. However, his mind kept traveling back to a small country on the mainland and a soon-to-be King. If he couldn't get his head back on the code, he wouldn't be able to take on bigger jobs.

He lifted his beer bottle and tipped it back, but nothing came out. He sighed. It was empty. If he didn't get his mind straightened out and fixed soon, he'd mess up a job, and his reputation would be shit. There was no coming back from even a single failure in his line of work—not as an independent consultant.

Malcolm was taking away his one escape: the job he loved. He tried to muster the energy to rise and fetch another bottle of beer, but he wasn't sure he cared enough. *What does it even matter? I can just lose myself in the movie… if I ever find it…oh, there it is.*

He tried to imagine getting pulled out of the Matrix and finding himself fighting robots. Would that be better or worse than his current life? A gun fight on the TV distracted him until a knock startled him out of the Matrix world. He paused the movie and glared. *Maybe if I stay quiet enough the pillock will go away.*

A few seconds later, he heard a key in the lock, and groaned. Besides him, three other people had a key to his flat: his landlord, Adrian, and his best mate in town, Conley. He didn't want to see any of them. Adrian should be back in Ixica helping Malcolm adjust and Conley…he wasn't in the mood to see his upbeat friend. He'd make him do something and sitting was about all he wanted to do right now. Not to mention, he wouldn't be able to explain his sour mood.

He leaned his head back and waited. As soon as the door opened, the clatter of male voices told him who it was. With a sigh, he debated trying to stand, but decided against it. Conley swaggered in, followed by Stan, and Phillip. "Right! Now, mate. You've been back in town a week, we're heading down to the pub. You've been locked in this cell of a flat and you need fresh air."

Finley rolled his eyes until he could see his friend. "I'm busy."

"I can see that…and smell it. Unless you want us tossing you in the Thames, go wash up and put on some clean clothes. You have ten minutes."

He knew the threat was real. He held his hands up and Stan came over to pull him to his feet. A cloud of his own stink hit him, and he realized his friends weren't wrong. *Maybe getting out for an hour or two wouldn't be a bad idea.*

After a quick shower, he dragged on a pair of dark-wash jeans and a rugby top for the local team. Once he emerged from his bedroom, his friends dragged him out, razzing him the whole way. He followed them two blocks to their favorite neighborhood pub, The Manatee's Kiss.

They found a table in a corner and ordered a round of

ale. Then, using some weird type of logic, Phillip grabbed the waitress's arm and winked. "Bring me a pitcher of that Jungle Juice you love to pedal—but add an extra bottle of vodka to it." He handed her some bills. She slipped the money down the front of her shirt and winked back. Suddenly, Finley worried about how much of the night he'd remember.

He sat with two glasses in front of him—a pint of ale and a huge glass filled with a pink liquid mixed with fruit. He drank the sweet jungle juice, it went down easily, and he realized too soon his glass was empty. It refilled and he sipped on the next round. Soon, his body felt heavy and numb. The room buzzed and he couldn't quite remember why its tilting to the left should worry him. Every time he put the glass down to try to think, it magically refilled.

Phillip draped an arm around his shoulders. "Now, Fin, Conley let us know about your friend's pa dying, and we're sorry. We get why you disappeared on us. Missed that concert we'd planned on going to together. You had the tickets, you know. Good thing Stan knows where you hide things."

His brain could barely keep up with what Phil said, but he now knew why his desk had been rearranged when he'd returned from Ixica. Damned tickets. Stupid concert. "Course 'e did."

"Now tell me, friend." Phillip's arm tightened, and Finley leaned over, dropping his head on Phillip's shoulder.

"What brought you back in such a state? Did you finally hook up with some lass and get your heart ripped out?"

His mind swirled with images of that night: Malcolm's hard body glistening in the shower, in the bed, them together. Anguish rose in him like a wave, and he couldn't stop his mouth from spewing out words. "Heart broken. All these years…avoiding…but couldn't avoid…it finally happened, but nothing. All for nothing. Why did I let it happen?" He wanted to take it back, but the words were out. He couldn't unsay them.

He grabbed the glass of jungle juice and emptied it. A warm haze covered his body and mind and he finally felt numb.

From a distance, Stan crowed with laughter. "I knew it! He's had a girl over in Ixica all these years he's been pining after. He finally wooed her to his bed, and then he messed it all up. She realized he was a wanker of a computer nerd and didn't want anything more to do with him."

Phillip, whose arm still weighed Finley down, gave him a shake. "Who is she, mate? A farmhand? A servant? Security? Does she work in the kitchen? Is that why you started to learn how to bake all those years ago?"

The room began spinning on a tilt which at least gave Finley the opportunity to stop talking. He tried to breathe to stop his stomach from performing a highly complicated gymnastics routine.

Stan chuckled and started jabbering again. Finley couldn't follow his friend's words, but Phillip dragged him back, so he wasn't leaning on the table. His head lolled over as a weight landed on his legs. The buxom waitress leaned in and tried to kiss him. At the last moment he twisted his head away and mumbled, "Not a girl; God above, haven't I suffered enough? I just wanna go home."

The weight slid from him, and he heard the woman talk with his friends. Then, his friends lifted him, dragging him through the pub. He tried to help as he half-walked and they half- carried him through the streets.

On his left, Conley grumbled, "Fuck, you weigh a ton. Now, Fin, we need to talk…that waitress said something about you not wanting a girl. Was that drunken mumbling—or have you always preferred men?"

His chin hit his chest and he groaned as the sidewalk kept tilting, trying to throw him down. "Is now time… right?" His vision threatened to black out and nausea rose.

Stan on his other side gave him a squeeze. "Sure is. Spill."

Slumping, he wondered if every one of his well-placed plans would crumble around him. "Yes…always."

Phillip, who led their rag-tag group, laughed. "All these years. Why didn't you tell us? You think any of us would care? See you differently? We already know you're a freak, Fin. How does this change anything?"

They'd made it to his flat and headed up the stairs.

Finley wanted to cry. His friends accepted him. When they reached his room, they tossed him onto his bed—which somehow caught him despite it running around his room in circles. Before they left, Conley said, "We *will* be getting the whole Ixica story from you when you're coherent!"

As he heard the door click shut, he wasn't sure if that was a promise or a threat.

CHAPTER 18

Malcolm sat on the end of his bed, elbows on his knees, head in his hands, the former pounding. He felt like a stranger in his own room. The designs hung on one wall and the fabric samples pinned on the board he'd been considering for his last few outfit ideas. They were all ready to send to Casimir. On the desk sat a pile of books and binders Sidney had given him to study. Every surface of the room had something of either his old life or his new, and he was drowning in it. Nothing felt like *him* anymore as he felt swamped in the paraphernalia of two lives.

Snarling, he grabbed an outfit for the next day, and left

his room. He couldn't fall asleep with all the angst fighting around him. He needed to purge what had been, move on from being a designer to being King, but the past anchored him. Once he tossed it away, he'd be admitting his dream life was truly over. If he didn't have his designs, what *did* he have? Who was he? Was he really the same person?

He stood in the hallway and wasn't sure where to go to find a free place to sleep. The American guests would be returning, so he didn't want to go to the guest wing. There were other rooms, but they hadn't been opened up and he wasn't sure the beds were made. It was late and he didn't want to bother any servants. Adrian had been correct; they were avoiding him—and for good reason. He'd been snapping at everyone. His emotions were in turmoil, and he needed to stop lashing out.

Holding his outfit and standing there like an idiot, he felt lost and alone. Maybe he could sleep on one of the couches in Adrian's sitting area, but then he'd have to explain to Adrian why he wasn't sleeping in *his* room. He wasn't ready for that conversation. His head continued to pound as he settled on the only made bed he could think of that didn't come with questions.

Spinning on his heel, he headed down the hall and across to the guest wing of the third floor. Taking the first door on his right, he entered Finley's room. He tried not to make more of his decision; he wanted an empty bed ready for sleeping and a peaceful room without the junk to aggravate him.

Finley's room felt cold without the tall, fiery man in residence. Malcolm dropped his clothes on the table against the far wall and began searching the closet and bedside table drawers. He wasn't sure what he'd hoped to find, but something in him settled when he found a few clothes in the closet and the dresser drawers. Finley hadn't left for good. Part of him feared he'd alienated the man from Ixica entirely. He knew his family wanted him here as much as Finley loved being here.

It's Adrian. I just don't want to upset my brother…that's it. If Finley doesn't return, who will put up with Adrian's antics?

Malcolm wondered if anyone would believe him if he tried to pull that logic over on them. He wouldn't believe someone who tried to convince him of that.

He sat on the bed, tucking himself under the sheet and blanket. His head hit the pillow, and he realized he could still smell Finley in the room.

Malcolm closed his eyes. Breathing Finley's scent eased the tension in his muscles. He drifted away into sleep.

The next morning, he showered and dressed. Outside Finley's door the corridor was quiet and empty. On the main staircase he ran into the first servant he'd seen in days. Her eyes grew as she spun to scurry off. "Hold up a sec, Tracy."

She froze a beat before turning back to face him. "Your Highness." She curtsied.

"I'm sorry I've been such a grouch. I wanted to ask that you tell the servants to leave Finley's room alone for now. I'll let you know when I'd like it cleaned."

Tracy gave him a small smile before dropping another curtsy and heading away. Malcolm watched her turn the corner before he headed down to the family dining room for breakfast.

Adrian was the only one there. Malcolm sat and the footman served him a plate of food and a mug of coffee. His brother smiled. "Glad you could join us, brother. You haven't slept in this late in a while. Good night's sleep?"

He sipped his coffee and debated his answer. It hadn't occurred to him until that moment that he *had* slept well. It was his first night spent without tossing and turning since before his pa's death. He actually felt relaxed and refreshed.

Adrian pushed his plate away. "You'd better hurry up; we need to meet with Sidney in fifteen minutes."

And all his good feelings fled the palace.

They entered the throne room and Sidney stood in his usual spot. "Your mother is at a meeting in the city. Prince Malcolm, please take the King's throne. Prince Adrian, take Princess Anastasia's seat for now."

They both moved to their assigned places. Sidney didn't move. "Prince Malcolm, you'll be expected to sit taller with your back straight. Chin high…a bit higher. Come on now, be proud of who you are and the country you lead. Just a bit straighter."

"There's nothing straight about me," he mumbled. A small snort came from his brother, attesting that he hadn't whispered softly enough. He rolled his shoulders back and tried to gain another few centimeters of height.

With a tight face and narrowed eyes, Sidney gave a curt nod. "You should sit like that at all times to practice. You'll need to see petitioners two to three times a week, and they'll expect royalty, Prince Malcolm—not a slob."

Malcolm pressed his lips tightly together and breathed through his nose. Once he knew he could be diplomatic, he forced a small smile. "Thank you for your input, Advisor Sidney. I'll be sure to take it under advisement."

Sidney's lips twitched. "Now, when petitioners come, they'll have to fill out a form and you will be able to review it beforehand. Even before you marry—and marry you will, sir—you can utilize Adrian as your advisor, or me, to guide you in your decision on how to handle each issue."

"But I don't have to, right?" Malcolm closed his eyes to take his next calming breath. "I'll have the power and authority to decide any of the petitions on my own, correct?"

Sidney's eyes narrowed, but Adrian answered. "Technically, yes, but you still have to follow the laws of the land. If you decide to forgo any help, you'll have to make sure to study each of the laws to ensure you don't cross some line. That's the beauty of utilizing me…or Anastasia if you'd prefer. We've both been studying the laws for years."

He decided he'd needled Sidney enough. He turned in his seat to face Adrian. "I can decide on either of you for my advisor? I thought it was already decided that you were next for that lofty position."

Adrian's ability to sit ramrod straight vexed Malcolm, but he decided to ignore that. His brother waggled his eyebrows. "You can have either of us, but until Anastasia and Jamie return from their honeymoon, you're stuck with me…or Sidney. At least, for these training sessions, soon-to-be King Malcolm."

"You're the one who first remembered and found the clause about the country needing to be led by a King, right? You ensured Ixica didn't get dissolved and absorbed into another country."

"That is true."

Malcolm nodded. He'd always known—well, since they'd told him he had to be King—he'd choose Adrian. He was good, smarter than the rest of them, but gentle in his lessons.

The next hour was filled with Sidney quizzing Malcolm on throne room policy and etiquette. He wasn't atrocious, but he also wasn't sure who was the happiest when the lesson ended. Adrian's gentle reminders when he faltered kept him from losing his temper more than once.

As they headed out, Sidney stopped them. "Prince Malcolm, I've tested you on all of these things before and you've performed much better in the past. What has happened? Is there something on your mind?"

He wanted to go, grab a sandwich, and lie down. He was tired of being around people, tired of playing at being King, tired of all of it. "I'm just…I don't know."

Adrian followed him to the family dining room where Malcolm requested a ham and cheese sandwich brought to his room. Adrian's face scrunched up. "You're not staying?"

"I just want to be alone. I need to decompress after that lesson."

"No, Malcolm; you need to figure out what's going on in *here*." He tapped the center of Malcolm's head. "Because right now, you're useless to all of us."

"And what do you suggest?"

His brother's face softened, and he placed his hands on Malcolm's shoulders. "Honestly? I suggest you figure out a way to get a hold of Fin. I don't know what happened between the two of you, but you've both been miserable, and it's starting to make me miserable. He seldom takes my calls and when I do get a hold of him, he blows me off quickly. All his social media has dried up, too. My guess is he's hurting. I don't know if you can fix this, but I think whatever happened between the two of you is messing both of you up."

CHAPTER 19

Finley circled the castle, the biggest he'd been hired to invade and plunder. If he could find a way into this sucker, he'd be set. He'd been inching closer for…god, how long had he been at this job? He did a quick mental check and realized he should feed and water himself, maybe take himself to the toilet.

Disengaging, he chuckled as he got up and headed to the kitchen to turn on the kettle for tea and then headed for the water closet. He prepared tea once the water properly boiled and quickly assembled a ham and cheese sandwich. Belly content, he returned to the fortress, ready to slip inside.

He began circling, measuring the defenses. On his last circuit before his break, he'd seen a loose rock in their wall, and he knew what needed to be done. Typing furiously, he slid the rock out, covering his actions with a veil. He slipped into the halls of the castle, tea forgotten as he lost himself within the code and the image of a rogue in a medieval setting.

His robed persona silently searched the halls, looking for traps and hidden treasures, paths, or hidden openings. Coming to the center of the labyrinth-like configuration, he found the goal—the point of this particular D&D mission—the quest's end. He activated the alarm the company set up to let them know that not only had he breached their defenses, he'd reached the center of their secure information hub.

After the alarm went off, he pulled out, patching the hole he'd found as he left. The company would be contacting him later once they verified he hadn't stolen any of their information.

He closed down most of the windows on his computer and stretched, his body aching from having sat in that position for...how long? He checked his watch. This job had taken a few hours, and he hadn't moved outside of typing and his sandwich the whole time. He shook his head and moved again as bones cracked along his spine. It felt like he'd woken from a dream, alone behind his wall of four monitors, his work cave.

"Damn, man, how long were you in that position? And do you *know* how oblivious you are when you get like that?"

Finley jerked then froze, mind unable to process what he'd just heard. He sat in his computer cave, in London… how could he have heard *that* voice? It was impossible. There was literally no possible way.

He stood up slowly and surveyed his flat, wondering if he'd finally lost it. Malcolm lay on his couch, reading one of his IT trade magazines. "Holy, hell, what are you doing here? How are you here? How did I not hear you coming in?" He shot a look at the door, but it was closed and didn't look broken, then he mumbled under his breath. "I'm never going to feel safe again; three times you've just walked in on me…bloody hell!"

During his rant, Malcolm sat up, a smile playing across his face. "You're hilarious, you know that, right?" He leaned back, folding his hands behind his head. "Hilarious and cute when you're flustered."

He trembled, not understanding what he saw or heard. Malcolm couldn't be sitting in his flat. Wanting to get to the bottom of this phantom, Finley stalked around his wall of computers and dropped into the chair opposite Malcolm and boiled all his arguments down to one word. "How?"

"You gave a key to Adrian; he lent it to me. He believes we both need to figure things out. He told me to fix things or don't come back…that second bit is rather seductive right now. Lessons with Sidney are not improving."

Finley raised a brow in disbelief. "He told you to not come back?" This really couldn't be real.

"Well, no. But I can read between the lines just fine. I know my brother and what he means. And why haven't you been talking to him?"

If Finley focused on the topics and words—and not the fact that Malcolm sat on his sofa in his flat in London—maybe he could survive this. Maybe he should've gone out and found some bloke to take the edge off his stress, but no, he couldn't do that. That had always been his problem; he wanted more, and he hadn't found any guy he wanted the "more" with. Only Malcolm.

"So, Adrian gave you the key…because I wouldn't talk to him on the phone? Did you tell him…um…anything?" *Does he know what he did to me by sending you here?*

"He knows enough, which is to say very little. But enough about him, I needed to speak with you and didn't think texts would cut it…or that you'd answer my texts if I tried."

Finley tried not to roll his eyes. "That's because I don't have your phone number; it would've shown up as spam."

Malcolm smirked. "Hacker hot-shot and you don't have my phone number?"

Of course, I have your phone number, I'm just not

telling you that.

Finley slumped, trying to ignore the familiar pain in his chest. "Why are you here, Malcolm? I told you why I left. Did you want to rub it in? See how miserable I am now? Maybe check out me living in the slums?"

"None of that, and I've seen worse than this. I just came to say that I've come to agree to your terms."

Finley forced his mouth shut before he looked like a complete idiot. He tried to get his mind to catch up with what he'd just heard, but nothing, literally nothing, was making sense. "My what now?"

Malcolm laughed and leaned forward, placing his elbows on his knees. "Your long-term relationship conditions. I'll agree to them."

His world spun out of control, and he wished he understood the rules. "Can you explain this to me like I'm an idiot? Because I'm sort of starting to feel like one right now."

Malcolm stood and walked over to Finley. He took his hand and pulled Finley up, then slid his hands to either side of Finley's face and pulled him down for a kiss. Groaning, Finley leaned in and deepened the kiss. He knew deep down this had to be a dream; he'd fallen asleep, he'd been working too hard. Malcolm couldn't have left Ixica. Desperate for any contact with this man, he took anything Malcolm would give.

When the kiss was done, Malcolm pulled away with a

smirk. "God, I missed that. I would really like to see how many other things we can do to each other that I've missed, or I could learn to miss when we aren't doing them. I figure this kind of testing could take, I don't know, years maybe."

A sound Finley didn't recognize came from his throat, and he forgot how to breathe. Still holding his face, Malcolm stared intently into his eyes. "Finley, my signet ring currently resides on a chain around my neck. The thought of wearing it gives me the willies. I would love nothing more than to take the God-awful thing off and slip it around your neck…promise made, never broken. Once back in Ixica, we could marry, then—when forced—I'll take the bloody thing back and wear it as King."

Finley felt like he was falling and didn't have a net. His hands shot out and he grasped Malcolm's waist. He still wasn't sure if he was awake, but he was leaning towards not. This was all too fantastical. He quickly looked around the room to see if there were any flying critters to prove to himself he was dreaming. Seeing nothing, he opened his mouth, but still couldn't get words out. A tingle running down his spin made him wonder if he could be awake, but this kind of thing didn't happen to him.

With a slow smile, Malcolm pulled him down and rested their foreheads together. "Finley, I'm afraid I'll need an actual answer to this question. It's a bit too big for me to assume anything, and I can't yet read your mind."

Finley laughed. "Mind-reading is in the next stage of Sidney's training?"

"God, I can only hope. Nothing else has been at all interesting. Drab and boring, all of it."

Shaking with nerves, Finley closed his eyes and asked, "Am I dreaming?"

Malcolm slid his arms around Finley's neck. "No, love, I don't think so. Though, I hope I am the man of your dreams."

"I've dreamt of spending my life with you, me on my computer, you designing clothes. In the evening, we swim or take horseback rides for ages…but then I always wake up, and reality crashes down on me. You go back to hating me." Finley tightened his grip on Malcolm's waist. "But, then again, we're still in the part of the dream where you're holding me; this is the good part. So, since we're in the good part, and I want it to continue…God, forever! Wouldn't *that* be nice? Yes, Malcolm. Absolutely yes."

CHAPTER 20

As they stood in Finley's living room embracing, Malcolm wanted to wipe away the years of pain Finley had put himself through to hide himself from everyone he'd known. If Adrian was any indication, his friends didn't know his heart, his parents didn't support his joy, and Malcolm had never given the man the time of day—not until his mother had forced them together.

If they hadn't spent the morning cleaning up that stupid room, he wouldn't have even known the real Finley; he'd believed the front the man careful constructed. *I wonder if even Adrian really knows him. Does Finley let anyone in?*

How deep of a hole has he buried himself in?

As he stood holding his fiancé, he decided he'd make sure the man knew he was free to be whomever he wanted to be. No more walls. Somehow, he needed to show Finley he wasn't playing, this was real. He loved Finley. If he had to spend the rest of his life proving it, well, it was a pleasanter task then most of his Kingly duties.

"No dream, love. And no more pretending to be someone you're not." He slid his hand down until he could clasp Finley's and led him into the bedroom. Finley's face was drawn, and shoulders drooped. After hours working, his head tilted to the side. Finley looked exhausted. Malcolm had waited over two hours for him to finish his job and notice an intruder. Even if all they did was lie together cuddling, that would be enough.

They both stripped down before climbing under the covers, and Malcolm, deciding to go slow may be better, didn't start anything. Finley on the other hand, didn't have the same plan in mind. Crawling up over him, he smiled down and practically purred, "So many fantasies in one day. I don't know if I'll be able to contain myself."

Malcolm bit his lower lip. Green fire blazed in the eyes above him, stoking the flames within. "Oh?"

"The soon-to-be King of Ixica in my bed, and this time I'm going to do all the things I've been dreaming of…are you going to stop me?"

As heat exploded deep in his groin, Malcolm's mouth went dry. He shook his head. "Wouldn't dream of it."

Finley leaned down for a quick kiss, then trailed his mouth down Malcolm's neck, sucking and nipping. He took his time, tasting as he went. When he got to Malcolm's chest, he looked up into Malcolm's face and smiled, "You taste every bit as good as I always imagined you would."

Malcolm gasped and his muscles seized tighter. His need for Finley grew unbearable. "What are you doing to me?"

Without answering, the man smiled and lowered his mouth, continuing his investigation of Malcolm's body. Once he reached Malcolm's cock, fully enlarged and begging for attention, he didn't disappoint. Electrified shivers of sensation shot from his groin throughout his body. His breathing became ragged as Finley found his rhythm. The pressure of his mouth caused Malcolm's eyes to roll back.

His body began to rock with the motion, and he realized the grunting sounds were coming from him as his ability to think and breathe left him. Then he fractured, his world exploding around him as pleasure overtook any rational thought.

He lay there as the after-effect of the orgasm pulsed through him, his body going slack with the release.

Finley rolled him over, kissing his shoulders, neck, and behind his ear, and he moaned. "I'm not done with you, Your

Majesty. You haven't been fully taken advantage of. Can you lift up to your knees? Or should I pick a different fantasy?"

Malcolm debated what he could do after a day of travel and the energy he'd just given up. He seriously wondered if Finley was trying to kill him. With a grunt, he managed to push up, and was rewarded with warm hands roaming his body, kneading and rubbing. "I'll fall asleep," he warned.

"Hmm," Finley mused. "We can't have any of that, now can we? I'm the only one here who can be asleep having a wonderful dream. You, Your Highness, are here to be used." And then the man slapped his ass, hard.

Malcolm didn't know if he should be shocked or amused, and he chuckled into the pillow. He gasped as something cool spread on his backside, and then pressure. As Finley pushed himself in, new sensations blossomed throughout his body, and he felt himself light anew with want and need. *God, how can I be this ready so soon?*

Once Finley's hips touched Malcom's ass, his hands slid around to grasp his cock. "Well, you're getting there— but not quite yet." His hands moved to Malcolm's hips, and he started a slow tortuous slide in and out.

After the second slow pass, Malcolm slammed back. "God, man, you *are* trying to kill me. Fuck me or don't, but don't dally about it."

With a full laugh, Finley began a real rhythm, banging in and out, his hands tight on Malcolm's hips and his breathing hitching as he went. Malcolm's body responded, growing tighter, the heat building. He reached down to stroke his cock in time with Finley's thrusts. His body began to tremble as the pleasure built. Stars burst across his field of vision and his seed spilled onto the bed below.

Behind him, he felt Finley stiffen, his fingers digging into his hips as he held Malcolm tight to him and released his own orgasm. After several moments of jerking, Finley slowly slid out. Malcolm heard him running water in the washroom while he knelt there, unsure if he could move. Utterly spent, Malcolm flopped to his side and rolled to the far side of the bed.

When Finley returned, he brought a washcloth and carefully wiped Malcolm clean before throwing the hand towel into a hamper and climbing in behind him, wrapping Malcolm in his arms. Satiated, it wasn't long before Malcolm drifted off to a deep sleep.

CHAPTER 21

Finley woke up and tried to move, but a weight pressed down on his chest. He thought back to the night before and wondered if the dream could really have come true. *Please oh please oh please don't make me go back to the life before that dream. I don't want it to go away.* He didn't know who he asked, he just squeezed his eyes tighter and held on to the last wisps of memory…just in case.

Taking in a deep breath, he finally cracked open an eye and looked down and the mess of black curls spilled out across his chest. His heart skipped a beat, and he tightened his arm around Malcolm, unable to process his reality.

With a moan, Malcolm curled in tighter. "Five more minutes, okay? Just five more minutes." He sounded drunk on sleep. Finley would give him hours if only to keep him here, in his bed like this, forever.

When he wakes up will he regret his words? Will he remember our past and decide he's gotten me out of his system? Did he really ask me to marry him? Finley squeezed his eyes shut tighter. *No more of that. Enjoy what you have; torturing yourself won't help at all.*

Muscle by muscle, he forced himself to relax and relish the time and sensation of the man cuddled against his chest. Regardless of what happened in the next hour, or day, he had *now*, and it was…a lot.

He must have dozed off, because suddenly the man who'd been sleeping a moment ago in his arms was kissing him. With a moan, he shifted and lost himself in the taste and feel of Malcolm above him. Suddenly, Malcolm reared up to straddle his hips. "God, you're addictive. We could lose a month in this bed and not realize it, but I promised everyone back home I'd be home by today…I think it's today. I can't stay."

A crushing force collapsed Finley's chest as he gazed up at Malcolm and nodded, trying not to let his disappointment show. Above him, Malcolm's eyes narrowed. "None of that, you said 'yes' last night, which means you had bloody well better be coming with me. We don't have time for this—"

He waved his hand between them and at the bed, "—until we get to the palace. Because I know you'll need hours to pack up *that*." He indicated the computer and the rest of the flat. "We need to be on the plane by…oh, I dunno, four?"

All the crushing doubt began to heal and foster a new emotion Finley wasn't accustomed to…hope. "For how long?"

An imperial brow rose. "Are you planning on leaving me?"

Finley dropped back, his mind spinning with more thoughts than he could follow. "But my life is here. My job, my friends, my stuff." He lifted his arm to look at his watch. "Six hours to close up shop?"

Malcolm dropped down and gave him a slow kiss before lifting up. He crossed his arms, leaning on Finley's chest. Their faces mere inches apart. "We'll have people who can come get the majority of your stuff. You need to pack that computer contraption of yours. We'll talk to your friends. Then, we can be off."

Finley pushed up on his elbows, forcing Malcolm to rear back. "We'll have…people?" He closed his eyes and shook his head. He still struggled to keep up with all the changes happening in his life. "I can't think with you lying naked on top of me—or with you naked in general."

The smile Malcolm gave him was wicked. "Well, that's good to know. We should shower, then I'll dress and see if your brain starts working. If not…well, I may be able to work with a man stuck in bed naked all the time. We'll see."

Groaning, Finley rose and managed to get himself into the washroom and under the shower. The area was small, and shouldn't have fit them both, but somehow, they figured it out. His mind continued to work at partial capacity until they were both dried and dressed.

In the kitchen, he started to prepare steak, eggs, and coffee. It wasn't his normal breakfast, but he was starving, and the food needed to be eaten or it would go to waste. He began to loosen up, twisting and flowing around the kitchenette, putting bread in the toaster, and seasoning the steak. Outside of the computer, the kitchen was a place he loved to work. Figuring out how to prepare food, seasoning, measuring, and timing, was a puzzle he enjoyed.

When he had two plates filled, he placed them on the table with mugs of coffee and smiled at Malcolm's shocked expression. "You can cook?"

He shrugged. "You should try my fruit tarts or chocolate volcano cakes. Baking was where I started in the kitchen."

Digging in, Malcolm's face morphed from shock to appreciation. "And it's divine. If you ever decide you don't want to become royalty, you can fall back on kitchen staff."

Finley froze with his mug halfway to his mouth. Just when he'd gotten his mind to start working, Malcolm stopped up the works. "Come again?"

Malcolm leaned back with his coffee in hand and chuckled. "You really are adorable when you're flummoxed.

Shall we take this from the top, love? You're returning to Ixica with me. You have my signet ring around your neck, and it's there to stay. I refuse to take it back. To remind you, that bloody thing is a promise to marry me…the next King. Once we're married, and I become King, what will you become?"

Finley's jaw dropped. His fantasies of Malcolm had been happening for so long, the inclusion of his becoming King had never taken fruition. "But…what about my IT work?"

"Now you're getting it, love. Misery so does love company. Let's pack up and go whine to Adrian and Sidney. It's much better when they're around to look down their imperious noses at us."

Mystified, Finley shook his head and finished off his meal.

CHAPTER 22

They debated where Finley's bags would go on the car ride to the palace. Finley argued that his stuff should go to his old room until they got everything figured out. Malcolm didn't like it, he'd just broken down the wall between him and this fantastic man, and he wanted to cement him in *his* room. But Finley's arguments were sound.

As they drove from the airport to the palace, they continued to talk, Malcolm learning more of Finley's past. After they parked, the staff did the transport, informing Malcolm that his family had just sat for dinner in the family dining room, and they were expecting him. He couldn't wait for them to see who he'd brought back with him!

He slapped Finley on the back. "So, ready for a family dinner?"

Finley froze. "You know, I've eaten dinner with your family for practically half my life—more if you consider how much of my life I remember—but the idea of heading to that room now…it terrifies me."

"Excellent, let's go!" Malcolm twined his fingers with the taller man's and led the way. Adrian knew what was coming, and he was really the only one Malcolm worried about. He figured his mum would be fine with it. Sidney would disapprove of everything. As usual.

Finley put up little resistance as they navigated the halls to the dining room. Before they entered, Malcolm pulled Finley in for a quick kiss. "This is going to be brilliant. I already know my family loves you."

They entered, their hands still clasped and headed for the table. Two seats were available, but they weren't next to each other. Adrian saw their hands and shifted to one of the open seats before anyone could say anything. Sidney sat slack-jawed while the Queen looked on with interest.

Malcolm bubbled with joy, laughing softly as he dragged Finley to their seats. Once they sat, servants placed two plates with Cornish game hen in a rosemary wine sauce, asparagus, and mashed potatoes in front of them. He relinquished Finley's hand so they could eat.

On the other side of Finley, his mum found her composure first. "Well, I guess I know what business you were concluding. I thought it was something else, but this will do. Are you going to elaborate, or shall we speculate for ourselves? I'll go with you caught Fin sneaking in to steal the crown jewels and now you're planning to chain him up…but before his punishment you'll feed him his last meal."

Next to him, Finley's face turned a bright shade of red and he made strangled sounds. Malcolm lifted his glass of wine to his mum and took a sip.

Across from Malcolm, Adrian's eyes narrowed. "You know, Fin, if you're going to be here permanently, you're going to have to learn a better poker face. You look ready to burst. Are you even breathing?"

Finley's brows came together, and he stared at his friend. "Really, Adrian, you, too? It's been weeks. When can I get off this ride and just have things go back to normal?"

A smile stretched across Adrian's face. "Friend, you left normal the moment you and my brother stopped pretending to hate each other. Now the fun really begins."

Sidney finally spoke up. "Am I to understand that there is something going on between Prince Malcolm and Master Finley?"

Malcolm sat up taller, trying to present himself in all his soon-to-be regal glory. "Yes, Sidney. I presented my signet ring to Finley, and he accepted."

Sidney nodded, his face a picture of disapproving neutrality. Malcolm wasn't sure there was anything he could've done to earn a different expression. "Very good. I'll incorporate him into the training. We'll determine which duties each of you will perform. It's simpler with a King and Queen, but this will work as well. There really aren't male and female roles. Oftentimes your parents would flip a coin to see who would do the tasks neither of them enjoyed." He pulled out a notebook and began taking notes.

His mum's gaze shifted back and forth between them. "You two look striking next to each other. Malcolm, all dark and mysterious, and Fin, with your lighter, less dour presence. Tell me, kids—when do you want to plan the wedding?"

Though this was the reason for his trip to gather Finley from London, he still looked freaked out. All the color drained from his face and Malcolm saw him look from his mum, to Adrian, then down to his plate of food. Finley picked up his wine and finished the glass in a single gulp. A servant helpfully filled it up again.

No one spoke while he had his moment. Malcolm watched Finley, amused, studying him. After Finley took a sip of the second glass, his head shot up, maybe realizing the room had stayed quiet, and quickly searched everyone's faces. Everyone watched him. With a groan he rubbed his eyes. "Is there a timeframe we need to fit it within?"

He really is cute when flustered.

Adrian laughed. "Attaboy, taking one for the team!"

Malcolm glared at his brother, but it lost something with his smile. "You call marrying me taking one for the 'team'?"

Adrian shrugged.

His mum nodded curtly. "I would love to step down, but in all honesty, we have some time…maybe a month or two?"

Malcolm stared at his mother, amazed. "I thought we had a year. Doesn't that give us closer to ten months?"

She gave him a challenging smile. "Are you telling me you don't want a honeymoon?"

CHAPTER 23

Finley was thrilled to survive dinner. After the meal, the servants brought them flan. The Queen and Sidney excused themselves. Once Finley couldn't hear their footsteps in the hall, he slumped. "God, this is going to kill me. I think I made the wrong choice. Can I return this ring, go home, and live in misery pining for you from afar? I mean, it's worked this long, hasn't it?"

Malcolm slid his arm around his shoulder. "So, you admit, as insane as this was, it was better than the misery of being alone at home?"

Groaning at his word choice, he leaned into Malcolm

in defeat. On the other side of the table, Adrian snorted. "Intellectually, I can conceptualize this, but it's still freaky. Fin, you're still my best friend, and the two of us *will* be going out on a ride to discuss…many things. You've been keeping too many secrets, my friend, and since I'm going to be your advisor *and* best friend, the secrets all end now."

Finley nodded and grabbed his wine glass. "Do I get any time off for good behavior?"

Adrian narrowed his eyes. "Have you been behaving yourself?"

With a laugh, he gave his friend a wide smile. "As much as I ever do, my friend."

"Then no."

"So, when and where will you subject me to the third degree? In the woods where there won't be witnesses?" Finley waggled his brows at Adrian.

Adrian leaned back and returned his smile. "Well, your life is no longer your own, *future King*." It felt like he'd punched Finley, and Adrian knew it, if his dancing eyes were any indication. "I believe your schedule will be presented to you in the morning. Training with Sidney, probably some training with the Queen, reading and studying the laws—you have a lot of catching up to do. I'll schedule an hour. Maybe after lunch."

Malcolm stood, dragging Finley up with him. "You are not nice, Adrian. I'm taking him away before he decides to slink off in the middle of the night like poor Jamie did. Once we're married, you're welcome to terrorize him all you want."

The three left the room, Adrian laughing, Malcolm smiling, and Finley debating copying Jamie's good sense.

At the top of the stairs, he turned to his room. At Adrian's questioning raised brow, he explained that, until they had everything figured out, it was easier not to make too many changes. About to close his door, he was surprised to see Malcolm had followed him. "Don't you need to unpack?"

Malcolm preceded him into his room and sat on his bed. "Not really. And I wanted to make sure you were truly okay. You've been stressed…well, I don't know, since we've not been adversarial. I thought I could just stay with you while you unpack."

His shoulders dropped and he gave a shy smile. "I like that. I don't know how interesting it'll be while I set up my computers, but…I like having you here. Maybe you can tell me about college or…something else. I only know a few of your stories."

Heading over to his bags, he turned to gaze at Malcolm sitting, staring at the ceiling, thinking. It occurred to him the bed was messed up. "Has someone else been using this room?"

Malcolm blushed. Finley marveled at the sight of his face turning red with an emotion other than anger at his pranks. Finally, the man fell back and laughed. "I may have started sleeping in this room before admitting to myself my feelings for you ran deeper than a one-night stand."

Finley sat on the desk chair and gaped. Malcolm shrugged. "Apparently, I was terrorizing everyone until Adrian pulled me aside to find out what had me out of sorts. That's when he sent me to you. He figured if he didn't, all the palace staff would quit."

Finley knew he should feel bad for the staff—he knew many of them and they were lovely people—but the story just made his insides tingle. He'd affected Malcolm that deeply? Standing, he launched himself across the room, pouncing on Malcolm.

Malcolm rolled them until he was on top. "You know, my mum did mention the price for stealing the royal jewels was getting tied up." He grabbed Finley's hands and held them above his head. "I believe that this would be by decree of the Queen herself." He bent down and captured Finley's mouth in a kiss. He pulled away and smiled wickedly. "We should build a dungeon, just for the two of us. Then I could punish you any time I wanted."

Finley groaned as his body hardened under Malcolm. He knew he should be unpacking, but all rationality fled his mind as Malcolm whispered plans to him between long, passionate kisses.

CHAPTER 24

Malcolm and Finley entered the library for their daily royal lesson. It'd been two weeks of this training nonsense, and Malcolm wasn't sure which of them wanted to run screaming more. Finley had set up his computers in his old room, but hadn't sought out any new jobs, hadn't really done much on the amazingly complicated-looking contraption. He hadn't had time.

They'd converted Finley's old room into their hobby room with his computers and Malcolm's old design paraphernalia. They brought in an extra-long desk so they could study some of the texts together, though that was usually only Finley, who seemed to be taking this becoming King thing more seriously.

With all of his past life taken from Malcolm's room, it left enough space for Finley to be installed in his suite, where he belonged. Malcolm had orchestrated the move while the other man had been in his first days of royal school madness.

By the end of the first week, the routine had become breakfast first, and then off to the library for their assignments. As always, when they entered, Adrian waited there, ready to help. Sidney, standing ramrod straight, looked at them disapprovingly. Then again, that was his usual expression. "Ah, Prince Malcolm, Lord Finley, you've made it."

It took a few days for Finley to stop flinching at his new title. It had been one of his mum's first decrees once their engagement had been announced. Though the announcement had gone out, they didn't spread it loudly. Finley had enough changes in his life; plastering his picture all over the country before the wedding wasn't needed. His friends knew, but that was it on his side for now. Things would get worse for him when his title changed to 'King.'

As they stood beside the librarian's desk, Sidney consulted his notes and didn't seem to care if Finley reacted to his title or not—that wasn't today's lesson. "Today, I'll work with Prince Malcolm, and Adrian will assist the young Lord. We'll work for two hours." He pinned Adrian with a hard gaze. "I expect our Lord Finley to understand all the land's laws, and soon. Prince Malcolm has had years. I've given up on him. I know Lord Finley helped you study and has some understanding already. Iron those out to a better foundation."

Arian nodded. "Yes sir, we are on it. Come on, Fin, let's stuff your head full of laws. It'll be fun."

Finley's face contorted into a facsimile of a smile as he was dragged deep into the bowels of the library. "You have a sick sense of fun, Adrian."

With a jaunty grin, Malcolm asked, "What section are we headed to?"

"We'll not be working in here today. Follow me." Sidney's face hardened as he led them out. They headed down the hall. "We're going to the palace archives. We need to make sure what happened to Princess Anastasia doesn't happen to you as well."

This confused Malcolm and he quickly patted down his body. "I'm pretty sure I'm male and will become a King, Sidney. What's the problem?"

He could feel the disdain as they reached the door and Sidney unlocked it. "What if the records mention the need for a King *and* Queen, your Highness. Have you considered that? I will not have a repeat of that international debacle. We've contacted Mr. Feile at the main Archives in the city, but we need to check things out here as well. We have some records that aren't stored in duplicate there."

Malcolm's eyes narrowed. "If this is so important, then why only two hours, and why not have Adrian help?"

"Two hours, because after that time your brain will be mush and your aid will be pointless. Adrian will be working on it this afternoon."

Malcolm sighed and got to work. Sidney had been correct, the work was slow and tedious. He kept reading, and eventually the words swam together on the page in front of him. He hadn't read anything that said there must be a Queen, but he wondered if words even had meaning to him anymore.

A hand on his shoulder made him leap. "Prince Malcolm, your time is up. You can go gather the others and head to luncheon."

Malcolm rubbed his eyes. The room around him swam. He rolled his neck to loosen stiffened muscles. He wondered if he'd aged a few years sitting in this room reading this tome. In the back of his mind, he gave credit to Sidney for knowing exactly how long he could focus on one of these books—but only deep in the depths of his mind, never out loud. He gave his temples one last rub before standing up and heading out. As he walked towards the library, he heard Sidney locking up the archive room.

He navigated the stacks of books, following the soft voices. He found Finley and Adrian at a table in the back. They had books and pads of paper scattered around them. It looked like they had done plenty of studying. He sat down next to Finley and sighed, staring at Adrian. "You are in for one hell of an afternoon, brother. Those records are horrible."

Adrian laughed. "That they are. I can't believe Sidney finally got you into that room."

Malcolm rested his elbows on the table and rubbed his eyes. "You know what? You're right. That's ridiculous. I've been behaving way too well. We need a night out. Let's go to the club tonight. Anastasia and Jamie return tomorrow, and things will get crazy again, but let's take tonight and just be free, the three of us."

Finley rubbed his back. "That sounds great. Getting out of here, dancing, drinking, not being called 'Lord.'"

Leaning back in his seat, Adrian smiled wide. "Have you even noticed what Fin wears out to the club, Malcolm? Have you actually seen most of his wardrobe?"

Finley glared at Adrian. "What? I like cargo shorts. The pockets are big and hold things. Lots and lots of things. I like things."

With a wink to Adrian, Malcolm patted Finley's knee. "Any cargo shorts that enter this palace will be systematically burned. I may make a new law. Now, I will take you shopping this afternoon, and then the three of us will go out and blow off steam."

Finley's look of startled terror amused him enough that

Malcolm pulled him in for a kiss. Across the table, Adrian squawked, "Just stop. I'm having a hard enough time with you two getting along, I do *not* need to see that. Just, no. I'll see you two at lunch, and we're going out dancing, none of…" His hands waved between them. "You know what I'm saying…on the dance floor." He made another strangled sound and stomped away.

Their faces were still close, and Finley leaned in so his mouth was near Malcolm's ear. "He said no bumping and grinding at the club, nothing about what we can do in the library. We could—"

"No, you can't. I don't care who you are, no canoodling in the library. Out with you both!" the librarian's voice cut across the room like a knife.

CHAPTER 25

Finley had been surprised when the Queen had agreed with their plan to take the rest of the day off. Sidney had argued, but she'd overridden him, explaining they'd worked hard over the last few weeks and deserved an afternoon off. She may have also looked askance at his clothes.

Once Malcolm had Finley in a clothing shop, he acted like a kid in a candy shop. They found something for the club, a few outfits actually—apparently Finley wasn't allowed to wear the same thing every time they went. But wait, there was more! For the small price of surrendering his cargo shorts, Finley acquired a new wardrobe, approved by the man he loved. *Do I really love him this much? Yes. Yes, I do.*

Back in Malcolm's room...their room...he had no other place to land so he'd better start readjusting the way he thought of the place, they sorted the clothes. Most of the clothes would need to be laundered, but they kept an outfit for him to squeeze into for the club. *How the hell did Malcolm convince me to buy leather pants? Oh, yeah; he gave me that twice damned look. I have to build up defenses against him. I have to build up a lot of defenses.* He fell back on the bed with a groan.

Malcolm called up servants to take away the laundry, and then they headed down for dinner. Finley ate without tasting his food.

Adrian reported on his day searching the archives. "There are five documents that aren't also stored in town. Malcolm went through one of them this morning. I went through two this afternoon, and two earlier this week. I really don't think we need to worry. The idea of same gendered pairings was outside the scope of the creation of these documents. I believe if the founders had considered them, Anastasia could've been Queen...or, maybe not. Who knows what the framers were like?"

Adrian smiled up at Finley. "You know, Anastasia and Jamie return tomorrow. Jamie will be working with me, and the first project I'll be assigning her is consulting with you to tighten up our digital security. I know it's bugged you for years."

Shocked, Finley gaped at his friend. "Truly? We'll finally be able to tighten up your firewalls and protect your data?"

"Yes, my friend. You'll be given a budget and everything. Unless you need a bigger space, you can use your room as your central hub. There's a room in the basement with more computers, but I'm guessing you'll want to toss them and start over."

Finley began to buzz with excitement. He'd always worked security from the other side, breaking in. It would be interesting being the knight instead of the rogue. Protecting the treasure room, not finding holes in the security to steal the crown jewel.

Once they'd eaten, Finley grabbed the red leather pants...or as Malcolm described them, 'deep wine,' and wrestled to get them on his body. They were tight, and instead of a button and zipper they tied shut. "You know, Malcolm, you're going to have to help me every time I have to use the facilities. I don't know that I'll be able to function with these pants alone."

Coming up behind him and rubbing his hands over Finley's ass and around to his crotch to linger, Malcolm whispered, "Trust me love, that isn't a hardship." Finley groaned, suddenly appreciating just how tight the pants were.

With a laugh, Malcolm backed up and threw him a top: a tight black mesh shirt with a white abstract image on it. He would've tucked it in if it were possible. He slid on black leather shoes, and he thought he was ready to go.

"Oh, no, love, this is your first time in the public eye with me, and no one really knows who you are. In the future, you'll head out like that, but for tonight, we're going to play." A shiver ran down Finley's spine at the tone in Malcolm's voice, seductive and playful.

He debated explaining that people did know who he was after years of clubbing with the family. This would be the first time they'd been seen as a unit.

When they headed down the main stairs to meet Adrian, Finley's auburn waves were slicked back, and black eyeshadow had been applied. He refused to admit he looked like one of the men he'd secretly watched at the club when he'd go out with Adrian in college or his friends back in London. He was shocked he could pull off the look.

Malcolm was similarly attired with black leather pants and a mesh shirt, but he didn't have the slicked back hair or makeup on.

Adrian watched them approach with a huge smile. "Damn, Fin, I hardly recognize you. Everyone at the club's going to be all over you. Is this how you'll look as King with my brother dressing you every day?"

Finley snorted. "Nope, I'm going to sneak off and buy board shorts and trousers with as many pockets as I can find. Only one thing was banned; I can work with that."

With a strangled sound Malcolm shook his head. "God above, what have I gotten myself into? I'll be burning your wardrobe every night!"

Laughing, they made their way to Malcolm's baby—his car, Sage Nightstar. Adrian got in the back and Finley took the front seat.

When they got to the club, the cameras flashed until they made it through the door. Finley had been through that before, having gone clubbing with the family often over the years. In his current getup, the reporters seem to take more interest in him.

Once inside, Malcolm headed to the bar and Finley and Adrian found a table. Malcolm came back with his famous drink that tasted like juice and loosened them up fast. A couple of women came by, and Adrian headed out to dance. Before he could turn back to the table, Malcolm grabbed Finley's hand and they joined the crowd, bumping and grinding.

Finley enjoyed feeling the music move through him. He swayed with the heavy beat; arms high in the air. Malcolm's body was pressed to his, their legs intertwined. Their bodies rubbed as they gyrated to the music.

Finley brought his arms down around Malcolm's neck and pulled him closer. "You're killing me tonight. One more drink and I may not care that we're surrounded by strangers."

With an almost purr, Malcolm replied, "Good."

The leather pants had no give, and they'd long since gone past tight and stretched beyond their limit. He licked Malcolm's ear. "I hate these pants. They don't fit."

Malcolm laughed and his hand dropped the test Finley's claim. "I like the fit just fine. By the time we get home you'll be in the perfect state." His eyes gleamed wickedly.

They danced close to each other for a few more songs, then Malcolm pulled him down for a kiss. "I'm going to get another round. I'll be back, love."

Finley knew it would take a few minutes, so he continued to dance, trying to release a bit of the tension built up from Malcolm rubbing against him. Another person wrapped arms around him from behind and he stiffened. Stepping forward and turning, he saw Jordan, the stable hand from the palace. Malcolm's ex.

Jordan glared at Finley, his face a mask of disgust and hate. "You're a stupid play toy of Malcolm's…you mean nothing to him. You're a passing fling. You're a flash in the night until he finds a true man to be his King…you hear me?" He started yelling. "You're a cum gargling glitter slut and I hate you!" He turned and fled, leaving Finley standing in an open area of the dance floor, stupefied.

CHAPTER 26

The next day, Malcolm and Finley went to the stables together. After hearing about the incident, Malcolm wanted to fire Jordan. Finley asked to be allowed to handle the situation.

Finley chose not to dress the way he had the night before, though Malcolm thought it would be apropos. Although they hadn't officially said anything to the household staff about their engagement, Malcolm was pretty sure most knew and today they weren't holding back.

At the stable, Malcolm requested Jordan's attendance, his usual pattern. When the man slunk out, he bowed his head. "I'm sorry, Malcolm. I was drunk last night, I didn't mean to make a scene."

Malcolm wanted to laugh in his face. The more the man spoke, the more confidence he had in Finley. *How did I spend three years with this man? Has he always been so spineless? Maybe that was it; he was infinitely controllable. At least Finley pushes back.*

Next to him, Finley took in a deep breath and sighed as if preparing for an onerous task. "You're apologizing to the wrong person. And I'd appreciate it if you'd call my fiancé 'Prince Malcolm' or 'your Highness.' As for me, you could call me 'Lord Finley,' 'glitter slut' isn't quite fitting; I wasn't even wearing any glitter last night."

Malcolm had to bite his cheek to stop from laughing. Not only had Finley called himself 'Lord' for the first time, but he'd called Malcolm his fiancé. It touched him, deep down. Meanwhile, Jordan's face was turning several shades of purple with rage and embarrassment.

Finally, the man sputtered. "That was *you* last night? Adrian's friend? But...how? You've never...you couldn't... you?" His eyes widened as all Finley's words registered. "Fiancé?" It was shot out with disdain. "You're to be the next King of Ixica?"

The stable emptied of workers as Jordan's tirade attracted more and more attention. Malcolm was shocked everyone didn't know.

Finley's mind must've been taking a similar route. His head tilted to the side. "Don't you gossip with the palace staff? Prince Malcolm and I have been sharing a room since my return weeks ago. I've been in training with Advisor Sidney each day. Are you simple, then?"

The head of the stable staff stepped up with a slight bow. "He knew. We all knew, Lord Finley. He was in denial. He was convinced if he embarrassed the Prince, he could win back his hand. He's been plotting it for weeks. We told him to give it up. His work has suffered since you've returned, and his obsession has grown. We've debated letting him go but wanted to consult with Advisor Sidney and the two of you before making any final decisions."

Finley licked his lips. "Give him one week to straighten up his act. If he can't prove his worth as a valuable member of stable staff, we'll remove him from payroll. If it isn't too much trouble, I'd like a report each day, or every other day, on his progress."

The stable head gave a bow. "As you wish, Lord Finley. It will be sent up to your office."

As they headed back to the palace, Finley turned to Malcolm. "I have an office?"

"You did great, love. And we'll speak with Sidney about your office." Malcolm laughed, dragging him back to the palace.

Later that afternoon, Malcolm parked in front of Casimir's store front. He continued to stare forward, holding the steering wheel. *I don't know if I can do this. Can I really walk in there as a client? Should we have called him to the palace? Am I being a wuss?*

The sound of Finley unbuckling his belt reverberated through the car, and then his warm hand cupped Malcolm's cheek. He pulled his face in and kissed him thoroughly. "You can do this. You're the strongest man I know. You can do anything, and I admire you for that. Now, let's go plan a wedding, and by we, I mean me, of course, I'll be making all the big decisions…pockets everywhere."

Malcolm laughed, their mouths still touching. He gave Finley one more quick kiss before pulling away. "God above, let you plan a cargo shorts nightmare of a wedding. I'll wake screaming just thinking about it. You'll have to hold me close until this awful image is stricken from my mind, you heathen."

He watched as Finley's face softened and his eyes lit up at his joking. Without thinking, he tucked in for one more kiss. "We have to go in or else we'll end up on the front page of some rag, naked in this car. Go!"

"I'm still mostly unknown, you know. So, the article would just be about you and some bloke. I may be fine with that." Finley waggled his eyebrows.

Malcolm snarled and swatted Finley's arm. Finley

sighed in resignation. "If I must." And he finally lumbered from the car.

They headed in and found Casimir sitting behind the desk in the main room. "I wondered if you two were coming in or canoodling the day away in that car of yours...*Prince* Malcolm."

Wrinkling his nose, Malcolm shook his head. "When we're here, and it's only us, it's just Malcolm, remember? I really hate the titles and you know it."

Casimir gave him a huge smile. "Sure. Now, how can I help the future King?"

Malcolm slumped. "Future *Kings* if you must know."

Casimir's eyes practically glowed and his hands came together in front of his chest. "A wedding! I get to put together another royal wedding. And you two look spectacular together. When's the date? What's the theme? Have you decided on colors?

Finley eyed Malcolm. "Can our theme be pockets?"

The horrified look on Casimir's face almost made the question worth it. They spent the next two hours hammering out details. Finley spent it on his phone doing...something. He gave a few opinions, but only when asked a direct question. Though Casimir tried at the start, Finley smiled and said he really didn't care, he loved experiencing Malcolm's world, for a few minutes. He was mostly needed for measurements.

Once done, they headed back to the palace, though Casimir agreed to join them for dinner to discuss a few more aspects of the wedding with the Queen and Sidney.

CHAPTER 27

Sidney finally gave them a free afternoon after a few weeks of King school. Finley swam laps while Malcolm *swam* laps. The man was a machine.

Anastasia and Emma sat in the hot tub and Jamie… Finley didn't know where she had gotten to. She had originally been sitting enjoying the afternoon with them, but then at one of his turnarounds he'd noticed she was gone.

He enjoyed the feel of his muscles burning with exercise after the time stuck in the library studying law, policy, and practices expected of him as a soon-to-be King. He yearned to go back to his computers and lose himself in code.

When Anastasia and Jamie had returned, he'd carved out a few hours for a few days to discuss what was required to fix the palace's lack of technology security. He and Jamie sat and made diagrams and lists, mapping out hardware and software and staff needed to run the system. Then they ordered everything. It was now a matter of waiting for the equipment to be delivered. Once it was, he and the three-person staff he and the Americans hired could set it up, configure it, and get it running smoothly.

His confidence in the new people was unwavering. Jamie's friends Emma and Tucker had returned shortly after Jamie. Emma was a wiz at hiring and staff management. She and Adrian had clicked when it came to running things. Tucker was oddly proficient with computers and IT; he'd also been on several hiring committees and knew great questions to ask. His understanding of people and interpersonal management was mind-numbing. Finley was happy to hide behind his wall of monitors—not that anyone would let him. Between Emma and Tucker…and Jamie, they'd built an amazing team. They only needed him for the truly tricky IT questions…though Tucker seemed to know a lot of that information, too.

He spent much of his time during lessons wondering how long it took to ship computer paraphernalia. If Finley was being honest with himself, his swimming was to release his pent up frustration at not being able to set up everything they'd bought.

"Finley!" The voice sounded annoyed. He spun and placed his feet on the bottom of the pool. Next to him, Malcolm zipped by. He met the eyes of an irate-looking Jamie. "I've only called you a hundred times. How lost in the laps were you, jeez! You Brits take this lackadaisical attitude so seriously. I've been on pins and needles with this first project."

He stared at her, wanting her to get to the point. *Do all Americans babble like this?* Chin lowering and brow lifting he could only imagine his message finally getting across to her. "Oh!" she said, bouncing on the balls of her feet. "The parts…they were delivered. Finally! Most are in the basement, except those few specialty parts that were put in your room."

His heart stopped for a second before the thrill of a new chase erupted in him. Turning at the wall, Malcolm smirked at him. "Go. I'll see you soon."

Finley made it out of the pool and dried off in record time. He scamped up to the third floor and to his room, wanting to set up his system first. The others could start in the basement computer room.

The boxes lay on the table next to his computer setup. What he'd brought from London was close to perfect, but to be a central hub for the full palace he'd needed a few extra pieces. He quickly began assembling everything.

He was on the last part, bent over to reach the back, when warm hands wrapped around his hips. He still startled every time Malcolm snuck into a room and he didn't hear. "Do *not* move, love, or I may have to punish you. Did you know that you ran up here without putting any clothes on?"

Finley thought back to the pool and his quick retreat. He groaned at the thought of himself running the corridors in his suit. Not his board shorts he'd had for years, but the new suit Malcolm insisted on, which barely covered more than tight skivvies. And then he felt that tiny scrap of material being lowered.

He went to move his foot, and Malcolm slapped his ass. "Don't move without my permission. This is my seduction. It's been days with us being too busy, and I'm going to have my way with you, exactly how I want you. Now, hold on tightly, this will be a ride."

Biting his lip, Finley shut his eyes, knowing what would come next. "We can't do it here, not on my computers."

The slap was harder this time. "I'll buy you new ones."

Finley groaned thinking of everything he'd lose and dropped his head to his arm. His computer was only a material thing, and it could be replaced…but it was his and…

He heard Malcolm move away. "Fine, move to the bed, but stay in the same position, and if I feel anything has shifted or changed, I'm bringing in rope, chain, and a riding crop."

Relief flooding him, Finley moved to the bed and tried to position himself in the same manner he'd been over his desk.

He felt the cool liquid being spread on him when Malcolm returned. "Now, love, you'll be saying one of three things. 'Yes, sir,' 'No sir,' or 'penguin.' No other words are acceptable."

"Penguin?"

"We're playing a game now, 'no' and 'stop' will be part of the game. If you *really* need me to stop, say 'penguin.' I've never heard you say that word…it's a safe word. Now, I'm going to fuck you. You'll scream; it'll be lovely."

Finley's body tensed and his heart pounded a staccato in his chest at the words. It was like the first time, all over again. His ass was slapped hard. "I didn't hear a 'Yes sir,' now did I?"

He gulped, trying to learn the rules quickly. "No, sir, I mean, yes, sir."

Malcolm chuckled, and faster than he'd ever done it before, buried himself fully in Finley. Finley reared up in shock and his body felt like he'd been electrocuted. He wasn't given a moment to adjust; the slapping sound of Malcolm sliding in and out and the feel of his nerves on fire took over his world. He started to shake with need, moaning and grunting with each thrust.

Then Malcolm slapped his ass again and he screamed, his body taut and trembling. "You're going to come for me,

Finley. I'm going to pound into your ass, slapping it," he did, earning another shout, "and you're going to release all over this bed. You may pass out from orgasming so hard."

Finley could barely follow the words, He pressed back, wanting more, needing more. After the next slap, stars began forming behind his eyelids. "Grab your cock, Finley…don't make me do all the work."

His hand shook, but he managed to move it from above his head, down. "Yes…sir." His voice sounded distant, but he got the words out. Once he touched himself it only took a few pulls before his world fractured.

He screamed again. He was pretty sure he yelled Malcolm's name, but he wasn't sure. Waves of pleasure swept through him as he tried to think, remember who he was, where he was. As his muscles contracted, he felt Malcolm's release, and then his weight as he fell on top of him.

In that moment, Finley wondered if there was a more wonderful feeling than having Malcolm draped over him.

CHAPTER 28

The day of the wedding was perfect. The days leading up to it…not so much.

The guest-list for the wedding had been hard to hammer out. Like Anastasia and Jamie, they'd agreed to invite everyone in Ixica who cared to come. That covered most of Malcolm's side of the wedding.

Finley's side wasn't so simple. He had three good friends who lived in London he wanted to invite: Conley, Stan, and Philip. The four had been good friends since college. That was easy. Finley also had an aunt and uncle who'd been decent to him growing up who he wanted to invite. But the real issue was his parents. By rights, he should invite them. But he had no desire to invite people who'd disapproved of him his whole life.

In a last ditch effort, he and Finley had flown out to visit his parents two weeks before the wedding. The one condition Finley had was they couldn't mention anything about royalty. In all the years he'd been visiting Ixica, he'd left that part out. His parents knew his friend Adrian was rich, but not that he was the son of the King and Queen.

That level of disregard disgusted Malcolm. Finley would come out for two to three months every year since he was a young teen, and the parents hadn't once done a background check on the family who took their son in? Probably was for the best; they'd likely ask for money or favors.

When they'd arrived at the small home Finley'd grown up in, Malcolm saw Finley's face grow tight with hurt and embarrassment. He reached over and took Finley's hand, giving it a squeeze. The house was run-down and ill kept, which confused Malcolm. Finley's father was a well-to-do lawyer. They had the money to keep a better house, but it appeared they just didn't care.

Finley walked up and knocked on the door. His mother, tall and lean, with the same auburn hair, answered the door. "Why, Finley, what are you doing here? You didn't call to warn us."

Malcolm stood in wonder as she didn't ask him

about how he was, give him a hug, or invite him in. For all the warmth and tenderness she gave, Finley could've been a neighbor or a work colleague from years ago, not the woman's son.

"Mother, I just wanted to stop by to talk for a few minutes. Is Father around?"

His mother looked back and forth between them. "Is this Adrian? He's so tall. In all the pictures you sent, Adrian seemed shorter than this."

Finley took a deep breath. "Mother, is Father around? I'd like to speak with both of you, if that's possible."

His mother's shoulders drooped. "In the living room; he's watching some footie. We'll pause for a minute. Would you like some beer?"

Finley led the way, and they sat together on a small couch. His mother paused the TV and his father grumbled until he saw them. "Finley, what the hell are you doing here? I thought you were off saving companies from Trojan fires, or some such nonsense. Too good to work with your family."

The man was tall and wiry with blond hair and green eyes. He sat in his recliner with a small table next to him filled with empty beer bottles and magazines. Malcolm moved a bit closer to Finley, letting him know he wasn't alone. *No wonder he escaped to Ixica every summer.*

Finley, who had been tense before, hardened more. "Mother, Father, I came to inform you I'll be getting married in two weeks. I am here to ask if you want to attend the wedding."

His mother's eyes widened in excitement, but his father's face hardened, much like Finley's. "Tell me, boy, why'd you come to tell us in person? What am I going to disapprove of this time? And how much would it cost us to fly? Get a hotel? Do we have to buy you a gift? Two weeks is such short notice; how long have you known? This feels like a pity invite for something you're embarrassed about."

Finley's head tilted to the side, and he started to smile, as if he were happy to have been correct. "Mother, this isn't Adrian as you guessed. It's his older brother and his name is Malcolm. He *is* from Ixica, and he's my fiancé. We're going to get married in two weeks."

His father's face turned red. "Not if you want to continue to be my son, you're not. No son of mine is a fairy."

Finley stood. "That's fine. That's what I figured. In two weeks' time you should watch the news, though; it may interest you. Or, better yet, after all these years, look up the people you blindly sent me to stay with during the summers." With that, he took Malcolm's hand and walked from his childhood home. As they left, Malcolm saw Finley's mom droop, a stricken look on her face.

It wasn't until they were miles away that Malcolm saw a tear rolling down his cheek.

Several days after that encounter, Finley's father had contacted the palace. Malcolm sent out the word to all staff that Lord Finley was not to be informed.

Malcolm called the man back to insure he didn't upset Finley again. Finley's father apologized to the Royal family, and Malcolm laughed. "You only show any respect for your son because he's to marry the next King of a country. When you thought I was his fairy of a husband-to-be, you kicked us out. Well, just think of it that way and remember you disowned him…things will be better for him that way."

The wedding itself had been nearly perfect. Unlike the ladies, Malcolm and Finley decided to walk down the aisle together. His mum performed the traditional words again, and they each stated vows that they wrote.

"Finley, I've known you for close to half my life, but until recently, you've kept me away with your pranks and tomfoolery. Whereas most of the people living in and around the palace thought you a hoot, I knew nothing of the warm, loving man you were. You'd erected a wall, and you'd become invisible—as you'd planned. Thankfully, that wall came down and I learned that not only are you clever, you're intelligent, caring, and a person I want to learn more about every day of my life. Your thoughtfulness will guarantee the people of Ixica will have someone who cares for them as much as he cares for me and the people in the palace.

"I promise that while you are spending your time focusing on making everyone around you safe and happy, I'll be worrying about you, my love. You've not had enough people in your life whose hearts were dedicated to making sure your heart stayed happy and healthy, and that will be my job from now until forever."

After taking a moment to collect himself, Finley tried to blink away moisture from his eyes. "Malcolm. I've spent my life hiding from the world, always worried that I wouldn't be accepted, be enough, be allowed to be the person I wanted to be—or with the person I wanted to be with. When I was young, I saw you and knew no one else would stack up. I knew then I'd built you into more than any one person could be, but to protect myself, I hid. Then the unthinkable happened—you saw me, you talked to me, you touched me." Laugher erupted then and he smiled at the crowd. "On my shin. But it was enough to turn my world from black-and-white into color. I didn't know what to do. You did live up to my expectations and more. You are every bit the man I wanted and hoped you to be.

"I want to spend my life proving to you that you are worthy of the crown. You are a good person, an amazing person, and you can do anything. You build up the people around you, making them want to do better just because they are around you. I love you, Malcolm, and am amazed every day that I get to say those words aloud to you."

CHAPTER 29

The wedding reception was much better than the ceremony itself, mostly because it involved cake and dancing…without leather pants. Finley hadn't minded the charcoal suits with the plum shirts Casimir and Malcolm had designed.

What he loved had been the cake-tasting and final cake selection. They'd ended up with three cakes: a lemon and strawberry cake with vanilla buttercream, a cookies and cream cake with coffee buttercream, and a chocolate cake with peanut butter buttercream inside and marshmallow buttercream on the outside.

They decided to postpone leaving for their honeymoon for a few days until all the guests had left. Finley had been systematically checking over the palace's internal defenses any chance he got. He'd been doing it on such a microscale it had taken him weeks. He'd found a few small holes and patched them, ones he'd easily have exploited from the outside. From his nosing around, everything looked clean and clear of tampering so far. It shocked him no one had taken advantage of such a tempting target.

Two days after the wedding, he woke up tangled with his husband. The words, 'his husband,' sent shivers of delight down his spine. Disentangling himself, he slipped on loose pants and a shirt and stole away to the kitchen to cut himself a slice of the fluffernutter cake…peanut butter and marshmallow, yummy. Then he headed to his office on the second floor and his computer console to continue his search for holes. He really wanted to get everything checked before they left.

He slowly ate while he entered his world of zeros and ones, mentally building the fortress around himself. Picturing himself as a soldier within the walls, he picked his next location and searched.

Each stone in the wall fit snugly to the one next to it, a complete picture of safety and security—but something felt wrong. This wall bugged him. He traced his digital hand over it and found one stone that was a bit off-colored from the rest. He dug in. It felt secure, but along the top edge there was a jagged bit that cut in; the brick wasn't right.

Typing fast, Finley slid the brick out, masking what he did so someone watching wouldn't be able to track his movements. In the wall, he found a compartment with documents, copied them to his external hard drive, and then put everything back, setting up a hidden monitoring system to record anyone who snooped around.

Once everything was back to how it had been, he loudly tapped the stone, making his action obvious, misaligning it just enough to show it had been moved but not removed. His last action was to email his team in an internal communication about what he'd done, letting them know to watch and track this area. Someone would be up, and they should pay attention from here on out.

His phone rang and he answered it. "Finley here."

"Sir, I received your communique. We'll be watching that area of the system. I'm not sure exactly what you did. Can you walk me through it and explain why?"

Finley looked at his cake and sighed. "Not right now. I'll call a full staff meeting in an hour or two and give everyone a full briefing." The staff was good, but he was better. They all asked him regularly about hacking lessons. In the end, the better they were, the more secure their system was. Teaching the three new employees how to do what he did could mean the difference between their security and someone getting in and doing…what? Finley wasn't really sure what a person could do in the palace's inner security wall. Very few of the sensitive documents were digital…not yet.

Sitting back, he opened up the documents and began to read. He ate the last of his cake as he skimmed what had been hiding for months within the inner code of their security wall.

His heart sank as what he read registered. Cold dread caused sweat to pool in the small of his back. Moving the information to a thumb drive and deleting it from his system, he put it in his pocket and headed for the family dining room where everyone would be eating.

He sat and ignored the plate of food and coffee served to him. Body trembling, he faced Malcolm. "I think I know why your pa was murdered."

**Please review to help other readers know
to enjoy The Royal Entanglement Series!**

**Continue to read about the crowning
of the next Ixican Royalty:**

Book 2: Tucker and Casimir's Story: Royal Coronation:
https://mybook.to/RoyalCoronation
If you missed Jamie and Anastasia's story, find it here in
The Royal Ring: https://mybook.to/RoyalRing

Find more information on my website:
https://hannahwillow217.wordpress.com

Find me on:
Facebook
TikTok
Instagram

Twitter

ACKNOWLEDGEMENTS

This book wouldn't be what it is without the people who read it and beat it into submission. Wes Imrisek, Elizabeth Daly, and Angela Grimes take my stories and make them more. The rest of my writers' group, the Confused Chaos, are there every day, getting me to laugh, write, and form better stories. I'll always be trying to keep up with C.C. Davies as she writes up a storm. Marleen Dekker and Kelsey Ortiz are the best beta readers ever. Fe Foster, Eva, Alice, Brian, Grant, and Jacinta are always there to help to refine my thoughts and ideas, making me a better storyteller. My son is always there to help me brainstorm new and crazy ideas as are the rest of my family when I suddenly ask off the wall questions.

I want to thank all my family, friends, and any of you who are fans of my writing. I love creating stories, and plan on doing this for as long as you want to read about my crazy characters and their lives.

www.ingramcontent.com/pod-product-compliance
Lightning Source LLC
Chambersburg PA
CBHW030959210726
48290CB00007B/2385